Puck Blocked

A Vancouver Knights Novel
Book 4

Kylie Kent

ISBN:
Ebook - 978-1-923137-04-2
Paperback - 978-1-923137-40-0

Editing services provided by Kat Pagan:
https://www.facebook.com/PaganProofreading

Club Omerta

Are you a part of the Club?

Don't want to wait for the next book to be released to the public?
Come and join Club Omertà for an all-access pass!

This includes:
• daily chapter reveals
• first to see: everything, covers, teasers, blurbs
• advanced reader copies of every book
• bonus scenes from the characters you love!
• Video chats with me (Kylie Kent)
• and so much more...

Kylie Kent

Click the link to be inducted to the club!!!
CLUB OMERTA

Blurb

Luke

Some things are off-limits. My best friend's little sister has always been one of those things.

Years later, I can still hear his voice in my head telling me not to go there. The fact those warnings are coming from beyond the grave doesn't help matters either.

Especially when part of me is hellbent on ignoring him.

The thing is, now that I've crossed that line, there's

no going back. Because Montana Baker is everything I've always wanted and can't have.

Montana

I'm not the same girl he remembers. It's been three years since I've seen him. Since I've become a broken shell of the person I once was.

Before my brother died and left me alone in the world... Before I turned to the wrong men for comfort... Before I lost myself...

But when Luke Jameson looks at me, it's not with pity. It's not with disgust. It's like he sees the old me.

I can't let him get mixed up in the mess that is my life, though. Which is why, despite how good it feels when he touches me, I'm already saying goodbye to the only man I've ever loved...

Prologue

Four Years Ago

Black. It's such a fucking depressing color. It's no wonder it represents death. As I look at the sea of people here, all dressed in black, a chuckle threatens to creep up my throat.

Sean would hate this. All of it. He would have preferred a rager.

I want to go out a legend. I want people to remember me forever.

Those were the words he once stuttered out. Granted, we were both wasted at the time. But now it's all I can think about. He wanted people to remember him. He wanted a celebration of who he was. Instead, the last time a majority of these so-called mourners are even going to think about Sean is today. While we're all surrounded by a cloud of despair, a ridiculous amount of tears, and a whole lot of fucking fakeness.

I've been best friends with Sean since fucking kindergarten. Our mothers were best friends too, before Mrs. Baker ran off. Which is why I know most of these people didn't even know the guy. They're here crying, laying flowers down for a stranger.

I don't get it. Why do people feel the need to mourn someone they never bothered to say two words to when they were alive?

A small hand wraps around mine. I know who it belongs to without even looking. My body reacts to the slightest touch. Her touch. It's why I usually go out of my way to avoid her. I shouldn't be enjoying myself, the feel of her skin. Especially at a time like this, when she's grieving the loss of her brother. My best fucking friend.

"I don't know what I'm supposed to do," Montana says, keeping her voice low. Quiet.

I squeeze her hand tighter. The pain I hear cuts right through me. I want to take it all away for her, but there's nothing I can do to fix this. "You're not supposed to do anything," I tell her. "You do whatever it is you want to do."

She looks up at me with tear-stained cheeks. "Yeah, somehow, I don't think what I want to do right now is an option."

This is where I should let go of her hand. Where I should walk away. At the very least, this is where I should take a step back. I don't do that. I wrap my arm around her shoulder and pull her against my chest. I hold on to her tight, knowing that once I do let her go, I'm going to have to really let her go.

"I'm so fucking sorry," I whisper before kissing the top of her head.

"Me too," she says, her fingers clinging to the lapels of my jacket. "I need you to make it go away, Luke. I need to not feel like I'm losing everything that matters to me."

"You know I can't do that, Tanna. I can't," I repeat, more for myself than for her. I know what she wants. It's what we've both wanted for a long fucking time. It's what I've been denying for years. She was only sixteen when I knew that I was in love with her. Two years younger than Sean and me.

I've never acted on my feelings, out of respect for him and our friendship. I didn't want to do anything to jeopardize that. I can still hear his voice in my head.

That's my little sister. Don't fucking look at her like you're a starved lion.

I pull back and drop my arms. "I'm sorry."

"You said that already." She peers up at me with a sad smile. I fucking hate it.

Reaching out, I wipe the tears from her cheeks. "You're not alone, Tanna. I'll always be here. If you need anything, call me."

She nods her head, but I know I'm going to be the last person she ever calls.

Without looking back, I walk out of the church. I can't fucking be here. It's too much. Instead, I head for the bar. The same one where we shared our first drinks together; the same one we shared our last drinks together too.

I wave the bartender over and order a Scotch. One turns into two, and then three. I don't keep track after that. Like Montana, I need an escape. I need to not feel the gaping fucking hole that's been left behind in my heart.

I didn't just lose my best friend. I also lost his sister. Because I know I can't be around her anymore. Sean's not here to catch me. He's not here to stop us from acting on our attraction, on our feelings. And I won't betray my best friend, even if that means giving up the one girl I've always loved.

When he was here, I had a reason to see her. To talk to her. I had a reason to be her friend. Because of him.

"Fuck you for dying!" I yell into my empty glass. I don't know if it's him, or the fact that I'm just that fucking drunk, but I swear the lights just flickered on and off as if he's telling me to get the fuck over it.

Truth is, I'm not sure this is something I'll ever just *get over*.

I find myself at a tattoo parlor after that. I had every intention of getting some sort of memorial tattooed on my skin for Sean. I wanted a phoenix with his name. Except, when I sit in the chair, that's not what I ask for. What I ask for has the artist questioning me five fucking times, making sure that *I'm sure* I want this on my skin forever.

Montana. The girl's already stamped herself onto my heart forever, so why not my fucking skin?

Chapter One

Present

My lashes feel like they're glued shut, my lids heavy as I try to pry them open while something hammers around inside my brain. I choose the option of keeping my eyes closed for a minute. I just need another minute.

As I lie here, the sounds of machines humming and beeping, the smell of antiseptic, and the coldness of the air let me know I'm in a hospital. They also let me know I'm still alive. Although these days I'm not sure if that's a good thing or not.

It's not that I want to die exactly. I just don't want to live. When living is filled with nothing but pain, what's the point? I've been trying. I thought I was doing really well.

I thought wrong.

When I hear footsteps enter the room, I slowly blink my eyes open, needing to see who it is, needing to know if it's him. My body relaxes and the breath I was holding comes out in a whoosh of air the moment I realize it's a nurse. It's not him. I'm not surprised, though. He's never visited me in the hospital before. I doubt he'd start now.

"Hey, darling, how are you feeling?" the nurse asks. The voice, it's one I recognize, one I've heard all my life.

"Mrs. Jameson? What happened?" I ask while bringing my hand to my head. It hurts. Badly. Much worse than usual.

"You were brought in last night, sweetie. You were in a car accident. Do you remember any of it?"

"A car accident?" Of course I was in a car accident. I do my best to not roll my eyes.

"Are you in pain?" Mrs. Jameson offers me a soft smile.

I nod. Because, honestly, right now I'll take whatever she wants to give me if it means the pain will stop. Although, there isn't a pill to stop the real pain, the dull ache deep within me that hasn't left since my brother died. Since I lost Sean and...

Nope, I will not even think *his* name. He doesn't exist anymore. Sometimes I wonder if he ever really did. I like to pretend that I made him up in my head, some fantasy a teenage girl created to escape her reality. But then I look at Mrs. Jameson, his mother, and know that's not right either.

It's on the tip of my tongue to ask about him. *How is he doing? Is he still hurting as much as I am? Does he miss me? Does he even think about me?*

I don't, though. Instead, I close my eyes and count to six. It's my magic number, and I'm not going to analyze why it's that number in particular that seems to calm me whenever I'm at my worst.

I hear Mrs. Jameson's footsteps head for the door. Then that little click that tells me she's left. But when I open my eyes, she's still here. She returns to my bedside and picks up my hand. I brace myself for what's about to come.

"Montana, sweetie, I've just read your file. This isn't the first *accident* you've been involved in."

"I've always been clumsy," I say without meeting her eyes.

"This is a little more than just clumsy. What's going on?"

"I was in a car accident," I tell her.

"Montana, I can help you. Whatever's going on, it's not okay. You don't need to let this happen to you. Please, let me help you."

"Mrs. Jameson, I was in a car accident." My voice breaks when I add, "Please don't tell anyone anything different."

"I'm going to get you something for the pain." I don't miss the fact she hasn't agreed to keep my secret before she steps away again. "I'll be right back."

When she walks out this time, I let a single tear fall. She's wrong. She can't help me. No one can. There's only one way out of this, and that's death. I know my time will come soon, and when it does, I'll be okay. I'll be with my brother.

I'm numb, staring at the far wall, when I sense someone standing next to me again.

"This is going to make you drowsy. Don't fight it. Your body needs rest to recover." Mrs. Jameson injects a clear liquid into the IV. I don't bother asking what it is, because I don't care *what it is*. Anything that sends me into that black abyss of nothingness is fine by me.

I jump at the sound of the key in the door. And rush to put away the textbooks I have scattered around the living room. I'm not supposed to have them. I was supposed to quit school.

I can't be a good girlfriend if my focus is split between him and something else. He deserves a girlfriend who wants to support him, not someone who only thinks about themselves. I know that, and I'm trying to be that girl. I don't want to be selfish, but I also don't want to drop out of school.

As I shove the books under the sofa and pull the cover back so they're out of sight, I stop and think. Am I like her? My mother? She was selfish. She left her entire family for a younger man. She did what she wanted without caring how it impacted anyone else.

Maybe Andrew is right. Maybe I need to stop thinking about myself. I don't want to be like my mother. I want to be someone people can depend on.

I flick the television to the news channel just as he walks through the door. Without a word, Andrew glances around the room before his glare lands on me.

I hold my breath, wondering if I've left something somewhere it shouldn't be. "How was your day?" I ask as I push up from the sofa to greet him.

"Shit," he says while sniffing the air. "I don't smell dinner."

I freeze. I should have started cooking by now. "I thought we could order in tonight and watch a movie," I suggest, trying to deflect the conversation to something more positive. I was so worried about finishing an online assessment I forgot all about dinner. Again, I was focused on myself and not others. "I'm sorry. I'll get something together now. Why don't you go take a shower? And I'll have dinner whipped up in no time."

He tilts his head at me. "You do that. You know we can't afford to just be ordering takeout. I buy you food to cook, not for it to sit in the fucking fridge and rot."

"I know, Andrew. I'm sorry." I take a step back on instinct. I know it's coming before it happens. The backhanded slap. The familiar sting across my cheek.

"Stupid fucking bitch. You didn't think. That's your problem. You don't fucking think," he hisses.

I step back again when he lunges forward. My foot catches the sofa and I fall to the ground. Andrew roars as he pushes the furniture out of the way and that's when I know my night just went from bad to much, much worse. I can't do anything but watch as my textbooks and papers go flying into the air.

"Andrew, no! Stop!" I beg, right before his fist lands against my face, the sound of bone crunching ringing through my ears. My vision blurs but I try to stay conscious.

I need to stay conscious...

I wake with a start. In a dark room. My heart racing and the machines next to me beeping just as fast. A nurse rushes in, switching a light on before she comes over to the bed. "Are you okay?" She presses some buttons as her eyes assess me.

"Sorry, I just... had a bad dream," I tell her.

"It's okay. Here, drink some water," she says while handing me a cup with a straw.

I take the water and look around the room. "Can you leave the light on, please?"

"Of course. I'll be just outside. Press the button if you need anything, dear." She smiles before walking out again.

What I need is a different life. *Can you give me that?*

No one answers because I can't bring myself to say the words aloud...

Chapter Two

The burn radiating up my legs doesn't slow me down. Coach has had us running drills all morning. He finally calls time but I'm not ready to stop. I keep going, working the puck across the rink until I'm the only one out here. Well, the only one skating anyway.

Coach and Gray stand off to the side. Watching. Fuckers are probably trying to psychoanalyze me. Gray knows why I'm not ready to stop. It's the same every year on this date. I need to skate until I drop. I need to work myself to the point of fucking exhaustion, because that's the only way I can escape just a little bit of the pain.

Four years. Whoever the fuck said *time heals all wounds* is a fucking liar. Or a moron. Probably both. Because it's been four years and it still fucking hurts. I'm living the dream, doing everything Sean and I worked our asses off to get. Everything we've wanted since college. *High school.* He should be living it up with me.

But he's not. And because he's not here, neither is she.

I let my mind drift to thoughts of Montana and immediately curse under my breath. It's the anniversary of my best friend's death and I still can't stop thinking about his little sister.

Four *long* fucking years since I last saw her. I haven't been back home, because I know the moment I cross those city lines, I'm heading straight for her. And that's something I can't do. Because, even from the grave, Sean is warning me against touching his little sister.

Ignoring the world, I keep pushing myself. That is until I skate past Gray and the fucker shoulder-checks me onto my ass. "You're done. Let's hit the showers."

"I'm done when I say I'm done," I hiss as I push back up onto my skates.

"You know I was hoping I wouldn't have to bring out the big guns, but you're leaving me no choice." Gray turns and waves a hand at the bench.

And before I know it, his six-year-old daughter comes barreling forward. "Uncle Luke, Uncle Luke, Daddy says you're coming over to my house. I made cakes. You want one of my cakes, Uncle Luke?"

I glare at Gray, who just smirks back at me. He knows I can't say no to this little girl—neither can he. "I can't wait to eat one of your cakes, Graycee." I bend down, scoop her up, and spin her around. "Are they chocolate?"

"Of course they are. Chocolate is the best kind." She smiles at me with so much joy, so much fucking innocence on her tiny little face.

"Okay. Well, I suppose I should shower first, huh?"

Graycee holds her nose and nods her head. "You're stinky," she whispers as I make my way over to the bench where her mother is waiting.

"See you soon, princess." I kiss the top of Graycee's head before passing her over to Kathryn.

Gray catches up to me in the tunnel. I don't say anything as I walk through to the locker room. After removing my gear, I jump inside a stall and allow the cold water to pelt my heated skin. I'm fucking exhausted, but not exhausted enough. Because as soon as I close my eyes, Sean's face stares back at me.

I've gone through so many different emotions over the years. Right now, I'm settling on anger. I'm fucking pissed that he did this to us. I'm more pissed at myself that I didn't know there was a problem in the first place.

I turn off the water, wrapping a towel around my waist as I walk back out to the almost empty locker room. Three pairs of eyes follow my every movement. Gray, King, and O'Neil.

"I'm pretty sure you've all got better things to do than look at my ass," I tell them as I drop my towel and pull on a pair of briefs.

"Yeah, I could be looking at my wife's ass," King says. Then I hear the slap that lands across his head.

"That's my fucking sister," Gray growls at him.

"*My wife*," King repeats, and I roll my eyes.

That fucker never learned to keep his mouth shut.

I'm honestly surprised Grayson hasn't killed him yet. When King first got with Aliyah, I thought for sure I was gonna have to help my best friend bury a body. But here we are, all fucking friends. Some of us closer than family.

I wonder if Sean would have been okay with it... if I had the balls to just tell him I was in love with his sister.

I pull on a pair of jeans and then a shirt, before I swipe up my phone and check the notifications. I have three missed calls from my mom. It's not unusual for her to call me today. On this date. She has every year since we lost Sean. But three times in a row isn't like her.

I hit the voicemail icon and sit on the bench as I listen to her message. "Luke, it's mom. I... uh... I need you to call me. It's about Montana..."

I freeze. Montana. Why would my mom be calling me about Sean's little sister?

I hit my mother's number in my contacts and immediately call her back.

"Luke, thank god. How are you?"

"Mom, what's going on with Montana?" I ask.

"She's... she's here. In the hospital," Mom says, then quickly rushes out, "But she's okay."

"The hospital? What happened?" My grip

tightens around the phone as I try to stop my hand from shaking.

"On the record, she was in a car accident."

"What do you mean *on the record*?"

"Well, that's what her chart says but I don't believe for a second that she was in a car accident, Luke."

"Why? What's going on?"

"I've read her file. I had no idea... Luke, she's been admitted to the hospital six times in the last two years. All *accidents*."

My blood goes cold. "You think someone...? Fuck," I bark out as my free hand runs through my hair. "Mom, what the fuck happened to her?"

"I don't know for sure, but I've seen this a lot. Too many times. Women claiming they're just clumsy. Girls who get into a lot of *accidents*. It's usually the boyfriend or husband and not a doorknob that really has them showing up all black and blue."

I see red. Whoever the fuck thought they could lay hands on Montana is a dead man. "I'm going to fucking kill him. Who? Who did it? Who touched her?"

"I don't know." My mother sighs into the phone. "Luke, she needs you. She won't let me help her, but I think she'll let you."

"I'm on my way."

"Drive safe," Mom says. "I love you."

"Love you too. See you soon." I hang up and reach for my bag before pulling my wallet and keys from my locker.

"What happened?" Gray steps in front of me. Blocking me from walking out.

"I... I have to go home. Montana's in the hospital. Mom thinks someone..." I feel sick. My stomach turns at the thought of someone hurting her.

"I'll drive. Come on." Gray snatches the keys out of my hand and I'm too numb to do anything but watch him.

"It's a three-hour drive, Gray. I'll be fine."

"I don't give a fuck if you'll be fine. Let's go," he grunts in my direction before walking out. I slide my feet into my shoes and follow after him. He stops to talk to Kathryn and Graycee for a second. I don't hear or even bother to listen to their conversation. My mind is reeling with all the possibilities of what could have happened to Montana...

"Last time I made the trip home, *to that hospital*, it was because Sean died. I can't do it again..." I whisper the moment we're on the road, my glare focused on the signs blurring by us.

"Did your mom mention how bad it really is? What kind of injuries?" Gray asks.

"No." I shake my head. "Just that she's okay."

"Then, she's okay. Your mom wouldn't lie to you."

He doesn't know Montana like I do, though. She's not okay. And I've been a fucking asshole for not checking in on her. I thought keeping my distance was the best thing for her, that I was letting her move on so that she could create a life that didn't include me. I thought she'd be happy.

"I'm going to fucking kill him. Whoever the fuck she's been seeing, whoever's used her like a fucking punching bag... I'm going to find him and tear his fucking heart out of his chest."

"I'll help." No questions asked, no hesitation. Just... *I'll help*. Gray knows all about Montana. What she means to me.

We went out drinking shortly after I joined the Knights, and he asked about the name tattooed across my ribs. Three whiskeys deep and I told him every-thing. All about Sean, what he did, and then all about the girl I was in love with. The girl I couldn't have. The girl I still shouldn't be thinking about.

"What if she doesn't want my help?" I ask after another moment of strained silence. I mean, what if I get there and she tells me to fuck off?

I wouldn't blame her.

"Since when do you care if people want your help or not?" Gray says. "Best thing to do is not even ask. Just do whatever you have to do to get her out of the situation she's in."

"You're right." I nod my head.

Montana is coming home with me today. Kicking and screaming if need be. I'm not taking *no* for an answer. I've let her live her life. I've left her alone, and now she's curled up in a hospital bed because some asshole thought it'd be fun to beat on her.

Fuck that. I'll never let anyone lay a single finger on her again.

Chapter Three

The door slams open and I jerk awake. Oh shit, he's here. He actually came. I can't let him see me looking like this. He won't like it. I open my eyes and glance around the room, my blurry vision settling on a male form.

"I'm sorry. I'm so sorry. I... I'll get dressed. I'll

clean myself up," I whisper, while trying to coax my body upright.

Everything hurts. I didn't bother to ask what my injuries were when the nurses and doctors came to check on me. I don't need to know. I just need to push through the pain and get up. Andrew doesn't like it when I'm not presentable.

A woman should always look her best, Montana. Are you a woman or a common whore? Because if you're going to dress like a whore, I'll have no choice but to treat you like one.

The memory of his warning rings through my head as I attempt to stand.

"Tanna, Stop moving."

I freeze. He must have done a real number on my head this time around. Because that voice... that nickname... Only two people have ever called me that. My brother and—

Nope, not going there. Luke is not here. He can't be here. He wouldn't be here.

"Tanna, you're okay. It's going to be okay." He touches my hand and I freeze. There's that voice again, that spark of electricity that zaps through my hand as his skin makes contact with mine. It's him.

"Luke?" I question quietly before peering up at him. "Am I dreaming?"

"Do you dream about me often, Tanna?" He chuckles, and I try to move again. "Fuck, you really need to stop trying to get out of that bed or you're going to hurt yourself," he says, his tone a little harsher now.

I stop while doing my best to sink into the mattress. "Sorry... I... Why are you here, Luke?"

"The better question is why didn't you call me the first time this happened to you, Tanna?" He sounds pissed off, and I try to take my hand out of his, which only seems to have him holding on tighter.

"I don't know what you're talking about. I was in a car accident." I refuse to meet his glare, choosing to stare out the window instead. "You didn't have to come. If I wanted you here, I would have called you." I know I'm being a bitch, but I need him to leave. I can't have him here. I don't want him to see me like this.

"I don't care if you want me here or not. I'm not leaving without you."

I still don't look at him. Maybe if I ignore him, he'll go away. What if Andrew does come by? What if he sees Luke? If that happens, things will only get worse for me. Luke doesn't get it. No one does. My heart starts beating faster, the beeping of the machine next to me just as frantic sounding.

"Tanna, what's wrong?" Luke asks.

"You can't be here." This time, I turn my head to look at him. "I can't... You have to leave."

"Who did this to you, Montana? You want me to leave? Fine, I'll leave. But I'm gonna need a name first."

The door opens and Mrs. Jameson walks in. "Montana, how are you feeling?"

"I don't want visitors." I plead with my eyes. Someone needs to listen to me. Needs to hear what I'm trying to tell them.

"Oh, well, um..." She glances between me and her son.

"It's okay, Mom. I've got this," Luke tells her as he pushes up from the little hospital chair. "I'm gonna go talk to one of the docs about releasing you. Then I'm taking you back to Vancouver with me."

"Why?" I ask, instead of insisting that I'm not going with him.

I can't go to Vancouver. I really can't.

"Because Sean would kick my ass if he knew I let this happen to you," Luke says, knocking the wind out of me. He's here because of his loyalty to my brother. It has nothing to do with me.

"Sean's dead, Luke. He's not coming back, and if he cared what happened to me, he wouldn't have died," I grind out. I'm angry. At everyone. Including my brother.

"Sean fucking loved you more than anything else, Montana. Don't you ever think or say otherwise. Especially today." Luke turns and storms out of the room.

"I'm sorry," Mrs. Jameson whispers as she watches the door slam closed. "He means well. He just... Today's hard for him."

Yeah, it's not a picnic for me either.

"I know," I say while keeping my thoughts to myself.

Today is the anniversary of my brother's death. The day he left me behind. Sometimes I think that maybe selfishness is just in our blood.

"Let him help you, Montana."

"I... I was in a car accident. I don't need help," I insist. Because if I say it enough times, it becomes the truth.

"Okay. But just... go home with him, at least until you're healed up." She smiles and pats my leg in that motherly way she has.

I could go home with him. No one would know. Then I can come back. Things can return to normal. Andrew won't look for me for a few weeks. He never does. After we have an... incident, he disappears before he pops up again as if nothing happened.

I can spend a few weeks in Vancouver. Let Luke get his need to help me, for the sake of my brother, out of his system and then return home. No one has to know. Andrew doesn't have to know.

Luke shoves through the door with a plastic bag in hand. "I got you some clothes from the gift shop. They're nothing flashy but sure beats walking out of here in a hospital gown."

I look at him with wide eyes. I don't know what to say. "Thank you."

"I spoke to the doctor. You're coming home with me, Tanna. I'll have someone come to the house to check up on you daily. But he says you should be fine." Luke pauses after placing the bag at the end of the bed. "You want me to help you get dressed?"

If my face weren't so black and blue, because I don't need to see it to know it is, I would be mortified at how red my cheeks are right now. "Um... no."

"I'll wait outside," Luke says, stopping to glance at me over his shoulder. "Call out if you need me."

Mrs. Jameson smiles at her son before turning back in my direction. "I'll help you, sweetie."

It takes a while, but eventually, I manage to get steady on my feet. And with a little assistance, I'm dressed in a pair of sweats and a hoodie. I must be losing my mind, going home with Luke. But it has to be a better option than being stuck in this hospital. And, honestly, I don't have the strength to argue with him right now.

Luke is in the room and by my side within seconds of Mrs. Jameson calling out for him. He wraps an arm around my waist and I flinch. I don't do it consciously. It's more out of habit.

"Shit, did I hurt you?" he asks. "Should she even be walking, Ma?"

"You want a chair, Montana?" Mrs. Jameson asks.

"No, I can walk," I tell her, then look to Luke. "I just... Can you hold my hand?"

"Of course. Whatever you need." He pulls his arm back and I feel like I can breathe again. I try to steady myself when he reaches for my hand. I really do try, but I think he notices my discomfort. Because his jaw clenches like he's mad.

"Sorry."

"You don't have anything to be sorry about," he says. "Come on, let's go home."

It takes a bit, but I'm slowly able to walk out of the hospital on my own two feet. There's a Range Rover parked out front. Luke leads me that way before opening the front passenger door. I'm holding on to the frame, about to lower myself onto the seat, when I notice a man in the back. A huge man.

"That's Grayson, one of my teammates. He took the drive with me," Luke says.

I pause, looking from him to the man. I know who he is. I, like most people around here, watch hockey. Even if I usually only catch the highlights after Andrew banned me from watching the game when he found out I knew Luke.

"You are safe with me, Montana. I won't let anyone hurt you. Never again," Luke whispers as he helps me into the car.

I nod my head, but I don't believe his words. It's also not up to him. Whatever happens to me is my fault. No one else's. I caused this. I didn't listen when I should have. I knew I'd get caught with those textbooks eventually. It was only a matter of time. I'm sure Andrew has seen to it that I'm disenrolled by now. The evidence was all over the floor after he flipped the couch. Which means he knows I lied to him when I said I withdrew last year.

I settle into my seat and close my eyes. It'll take us three hours to make it to Vancouver. If I at least pretend to be asleep, I won't have to talk. Because, right now, I don't want to talk to anyone.

Chapter Four

I pull in the driveway and turn to glance at Montana. She's asleep in the passenger seat. She looks peaceful, if you can get past the broken nose and all the bruises that cover her face and neck. The asshole choked her. His fucking hands are imprinted on her throat

I open and close my fists, trying to gain some control over the burning rage that's running through me as I quietly push open the door.

"Come on," Gray says, grabbing my attention as he slides out of the back seat.

I climb out and gently close the door again, not wanting to wake her just yet. I turn to Gray. "I need to know who did this to her. She won't tell me."

"Already on it. I've sent her details to Vinny. He'll get a dossier back to me within the next couple of days."

"Thank you." I look back to the car. "I don't know what the fuck I'm doing here. How do I help her?"

"You've got this, man. You love that girl, even if you won't allow yourself to accept it. Just make sure she knows she's not alone. Remind her she has options," Gray says.

He's right. I do love her, but that's never been in question. I need to be her friend right now. All I can think about is how I've let her down. How I've let Sean down too. "Thanks for coming. You should get home."

"You sure? I can stick around for a bit," Gray offers.

"Nah, I've got this. Go home to your family. I'll see you in the morning."

"Let me know if you need anything." He nods his head and continues along the driveway. He only lives a couple of houses down, which is convenient right now, considering he left his car back at the arena.

I walk around to the passenger door. Open it and lean in as I unbuckle Montana. I'm about to pick her up when I stop myself. "Tanna, we're home," I whisper before taking a step back to give her space.

It hasn't gone unnoticed that she doesn't like to be touched, which just pisses me off more, because she'd always leaned into my hugs before. She was the one who held my hand through Sean's funeral.

Her lashes flutter open and she looks around, seemingly confused, before those big blue eyes land on mine. "I didn't mean to fall asleep."

"It's okay. Come on, let's get you inside." I take another step back and hold out a hand. After a moment of looking at it, she finally places her palm in mine and I help her out of the car.

Once we're inside, Montana peers up and then glances around the foyer. "Do you live here alone?" she asks while tugging her hand free. She then shuffles back to put more space between us.

"Yeah, it's just me here, Tanna. Who would I live with?"

"I don't know. A girlfriend, a wife?" she suggests.

"I don't have a girlfriend. And you'd be the first one to know if I had a wife." *Because you're the only one I could see myself settling down with.* I don't say that part aloud. Instead, I gesture an arm in front of us and urge her to follow me. "Come on, I'll show you the guest room. You okay to do the stairs? Want me to carry you?"

"I can do it."

And she does. Slowly, so fucking slowly. I can see how much pain she's in, but I wait right next to her, ready to step in and catch her if she falls.

By the time we get to the top landing, Montana looks ready to collapse. "You don't have to be okay, you know. If you need help, I'm here to help you."

"I know," she says, but I don't think she does know.

I open the door to the guest room located right next to my bedroom, walk in, and wait. "If there's anything you need, just let me know and I'll get it for you," I tell her while pulling the blankets back on the bed. "Jump in. I'm going to go and make you something to eat." I point to the door that leads to the adjoining bathroom. "Oh, and the bathroom's just through there."

Montana nods her head in acknowledgement. I watch her for a moment, making sure she's able to climb onto the bed. Then I run back down the stairs, skipping over a few steps along the way.

I want to pick her up and hold her close. I want her to know just how much she's loved. Remind her that she's not alone in the world the way she seems to think she is. But all of that would be more for me right now. To help ease some of my guilt. What she needs is for me to be patient. To not give up on her, like Gray said.

I tug open the fridge and quickly pull out some ham, cheese, and butter. I'll make her a sandwich. It's not much, but it's something. Next, I set the kettle to boil and grab a tea bag down from the top cabinet. She used to love peppermint tea. I started drinking it myself after Sean's funeral. After I walked away from her. It was a little piece of her I could have with me all the time.

When I walk back into the room, she's not in the bed. I set the plate and cup on the nightstand and walk over to the bathroom door. Knocking lightly. "You okay in there, Tanna?"

"I'll be right out," she replies from the other side.

"Okay, I left a sandwich and a cup of tea on the nightstand for you. I'll be in the room right next to this one. If you need anything, just give me a shout," I tell her.

Then I walk into my bedroom and straight into the shower. I want to stay with her but I don't want to crowd her either. If she needs space, then I'll give her as much space as I can bear to give her.

It's not until I'm standing under the stream of cold water that the panic sinks in. Fuck. I turn off the shower, pat myself down with a towel, and throw on a pair of sweats. Just before I walk out, I grab a shirt and chuck it over my head.

I shouldn't have left her in that bathroom. She wouldn't, would she?

No. She's not Sean. I have to remind myself that she's not him. She's not going to hurt herself.

Not when she has someone else to do it for her.

I tuck that thought away for another day and breathe a sigh of relief when I find Montana lying on the bed in my guest room. "You didn't eat."

"I'm not hungry."

"You need to eat something, Montana. Just try it." I pick up the plate and hold it out to her. "Please."

She pushes herself up, and it takes everything in

41

me not to help her. I let her do it herself though. She reaches for the plate and takes a small bite out of one half of the sandwich.

"Peppermint tea still your go-to?" I ask, noticing the cup hasn't been touched either.

"You remember that?"

"I remember everything about you, Tanna," I admit.

"It's been years, Luke. I wouldn't expect you to remember anything."

"We spent our lives growing up together. That's not something I'd forget." I lower my ass onto the floor, positioning myself right next to the bed. "Are you going to tell me who did that to your throat now?" The question tumbles out of my mouth without me meaning to.

"I told you I was in a car accident," she says, but she won't look at me. Something keeps her from being able to lie to my face.

"I'm not buying that. Besides, you don't end up with handprints around your neck from a car accident." I point out the obvious.

"I don't want you to do anything, Luke. I'm going to stay here until I'm better, and then I'll get out of your hair. I'll go home."

"You're not going back, Tanna. I don't care if I

have to lock you in this damn house. I'm not letting you go back to the fucker who did *that*." I gesture a hand towards her face.

She wants to go back. Is she fucking out of her mind?

"I can't stay here," Montana says. "I have... responsibilities. I have a life."

"Being used as some asshole's punching bag isn't a life, Tanna. Why didn't you call me sooner? This isn't the first time this has happened, is it?" I already know the answer, but I'd like to hear it from her.

She doesn't respond, holding out the plate to me instead. "I'm really tired."

I take it and set it on the nightstand. "Just... I mean, you're not... You don't want to...?"

Fuck, how the fuck do I ask this?

"No." She sighs. "I'm not going to try to hurt myself. I wouldn't do that," she says before adding, "I'm not my brother."

"I know you're not him. Trust me, I know." I peer up at her from the floor. "I miss him, but truth is... I think I miss you more, and that makes me feel like the shiftiest fucking friend in the world, Tanna."

"You are far from a shitty friend. Sean was lucky to have you."

"You have me too, Tanna."

She nods her head but doesn't say anything.

I wait until the silence starts to choke me. Then I push to my feet and make my way over to the door. I leave it open wide and then do the same with mine. Before I climb into bed. I'm fucking exhausted but I know I'm not getting an ounce of sleep tonight. Not with Montana in the room next to me. So close yet so far.

Chapter Five

"**D**id you really think you could hide from me?" Andrew yanks at my hair, and my head snaps backwards at an angle no one's neck should be in.

"I didn't... I'm sorry." I push up on my tiptoes in

an attempt to ease some of the tension on my scalp. It doesn't help. Andrew just pulls tighter.

"You didn't? What the fuck did I tell you, Montana?" The back of his hand lands across my cheek before he tosses me to the ground like a rag doll.

I land on my hip, on an already healing bruise, and wince when a sharp pain travels up my side. "I... I..." I don't know what he wants me to say. I need to figure out the right thing to say, how to get myself out of this mess. I knew I should have just gone home.

"You what? Just wanted to whore around with some hotshot hockey player? Be the next puck bunny in his bed? He doesn't want you, Montana. No one wants you. You're pathetic. I mean, just look at you." Andrew kicks me in the stomach, and I curl in on myself to help lessen some of the blow.

"No... Please stop," I cry out. "Andrew, please, I didn't mean to. I'm sorry."

"You're sorry? You're always fucking sorry, Montana," he hisses back at me.

"Tanna, wake up," a familiar voice calls out to me. I look around the dark room. Why is Luke here? "Montana, it's just a dream. Wake up."

I gasp as my eyes snap open. Someone is screaming. Not someone. Me. I'm screaming.

"It's okay. I've got you. You're safe," Luke repeats over and over again.

I peer up at him. The screaming stops, and the tears start as my eyes bounce from surface to surface in a room I don't recognize. He was here. Andrew was here. Where did he go?

"Tanna, you're okay. I've got you," Luke says again, and then I'm being lifted.

"What are you doing?" I ask, only just realizing he's not wearing a shirt when my hand lands on his bare chest.

"Taking you to my room. I'm not letting you sleep alone," he says as he sets me on a bed I'm assuming is his. Everything smells like him.

I freeze when he climbs in next to me and then pulls the covers up over both of us. "What are you doing?"

"Being the friend I should have been the last four years." His hand reaches out and wraps around mine. "I'm not going anywhere, Tanna. I've got you now and no one is going to hurt you again. I swear it."

I know he believes what he says, but *I* can't. I don't have that luxury. I can't fall into that trap. I've tried to leave Andrew before, and that didn't turn out too well for me. It's not going to be any different now.

"I don't think Sean would approve of me being in your bed," I whisper to the silent room.

"Sean's not here. And, honestly, right now I don't give a fuck. I'm not leaving you alone."

I let Luke's words wash over me. This is the first time he's ever said he didn't care what my brother would think. Does he mean it?

"Do you ever think about what he'd be doing if he were still here?"

"I try not to," Luke says. "I wish I knew... I wish I could have helped him."

"Nobody knew what he was going to do." I sigh. "There were no signs. I know everyone thinks there were. That it should have been obvious. But there was nothing. I've gone over those last few months, and I still can't pinpoint a single moment that indicated he was struggling."

"I lived with the guy. He hid it good, Tanna," Luke says. "I never would have thought..."

"Yeah... me either."

"Try to sleep." Luke squeezes my hand a little before he drops it. I reach back out and take hold of his palm again. I don't want to let go.

"It's weird, but when I'm holding your hand, I feel.... a kind of peace," I admit.

"It's not weird, and you can hold my hand as much as you want, Tanna." He shifts a little closer to me on the bed.

I close my eyes and release a long breath. "Thank you."

"Montana..."

"Mmm," I moan, rolling over and burying myself into the covers more. Every part of me hurts when I move, so I stop and just lie here instead.

"I have to go to morning skate," Luke whispers, and I open my eyes. I didn't even feel him get up.

"Okay. You want me to..." I don't know what I'm asking. I don't know what he wants me to do.

"Go back to sleep," Luke says. "I'll be a few

hours, but I have Gray's sister stopping by to bring you some clothes."

"You don't have to do that," I tell him as I try to push up from the mattress. My arms are useless and I don't get anywhere.

"I want to," Luke says, then adds, "Are you going to be okay, Tanna? Do ya want to come to the rink with me? Or I could call Coach and tell him I'm sick?"

"No. Go. I'll be fine. Besides, I can't snoop through all your things with you standing here." I grin into the pillow and finally manage to turn over to look at him. "I didn't mean that. I won't snoop. Sorry, bad joke. I won't touch a thing. Promise." Sometimes it's easy to fall into bad habits. Like saying things I don't mean. Especially with Luke around. He reminds me of the girl I used to be. A liar, according to Andrew. And I don't want to be a liar.

"Tanna, you can snoop to your heart's content. I don't keep any secrets from you," Luke says.

"I won't snoop." I shake my head from side to side and instantly regret it. My temples are pounding.

"I'll be back as soon as practice is over."

"Okay."

Luke gently closes the door and I try to go back to sleep, but it's pointless. After about thirty minutes of lying in his bed, I get up. Walk into his bathroom and turn on the shower. It takes a bit of time and effort to peel myself out of my clothes.

When I finally do, I look into the mirror and gasp. I'm used to seeing all the marks. But right now, my entire torso is a rainbow of colors. From red, where some of my capillaries have been ruptured, to a dark purple almost black, where the deepest bruises have set in. My neck is outlined in fresh handprints and my face, well, it's worse.

I turn away, step under the warm water streaming from the showerhead, and let it soothe my aching muscles. Then I squirt some of Luke's shower gel onto my hands and wash everywhere. I want to smell like him. It's calming.

After I'm as clean as I can get myself, I turn off the water and gently pat my body dry. This isn't the first time I've had to recover, and it probably won't be the last. What I do know is the more I force myself to move around, the quicker I'll heal. Lying down all day will just make my muscles stiffer, sorer.

I glance at the sweats and hoodie from the gift shop piled up on the ground where I left them and am reminded that I don't have anything else to wear.

But I can't just help myself to Luke's closet. So I decide to put those back on. It's safer.

As soon as I'm dressed, I shuffle out of the bathroom and over to the bed. Where I smooth out the sheets and readjust the comforter. Then I do the same in the guest room before I pick up the cup and plate and walk them downstairs.

It takes me a good five minutes to find my way to the kitchen. This house is huge, with a freaking maze of hallways and doors. I drop the unwanted sandwich into the trash can and wash the plate. As I'm tipping the leftover tea down the sink, I spot a note on the counter. It has my name on it so I pick it up and turn it over.

> Tanna,
>
> I left the kettle hot. Tea bags are in the top left cabinet and there's a plate of fruit in the fridge. Please eat something. Help yourself to whatever else you may want.
>
> — L

After making myself a cup of tea, I find the plate of fruit in the fridge and pick at it. The sound of heels clicking on the marble floor has me freezing to the spot. Someone's here. But at least that someone isn't Andrew. I know what his steps sound like. The sound is ingrained in my nightmares. I glance up just as a beautiful brunette appears in the kitchen.

"Oh, sorry. I thought you might be asleep still," the woman says. "I'm Aliyah, Grayson Monroe's sister. Luke asked me to drop some things off."

"Oh, hi. I'm... uh... Montana." I grin awkwardly. The swelling on my face makes it hard to smile.

"Well, I'm glad you're awake. I wanted to meet you."

"You did?"

"Oh, I've wanted to meet you for years." She laughs. "Now, is the kettle still hot?" She doesn't wait for an answer before she pulls down a mug and a tea bag, knowing exactly where to find everything.

"How long have you known Luke?"

"Since he signed with the Knights. Luke and Gray have had this whole bromance thing going on since day one." She hums as she pours hot water into her mug. "But you've known him forever, right?"

"Our mothers were friends, and my brother and Luke were inseparable." I can't help but watch her. Everything about the woman screams confidence.

"And you and Luke?" Aliyah raises her eyebrows

in question, and I drop my eyes to the plate of fruit when I realize she caught me staring.

"We were friends because of Sean." I shrug.

"Mmm, okay. Well, I have a brand-new wardrobe for you. From the looks of it, Luke did a good job guessing your size."

"You didn't have to do that. I'm sorry."

"Please, spending someone else's money is like my favorite thing to do. Just ask my husband." She laughs.

My eyes widen. Of course he's spending money. How else does someone get new clothes? Shit. I don't know how I'm going to be able to repay him. I'll have to think of something. Maybe find a side job while I'm here in Vancouver.

"Don't worry about it. I've seen his contract. He can afford it, trust me," Aliyah says, almost like she can read my mind.

When I don't say anything in return, she continues talking. Filling in the silence. It doesn't take me long to feel more comfortable around her. She even gets me to agree to watch a movie with her before she grabs my arm and drags me into the theater room.

Chapter Six

Practice was brutal. Even worse than what I put myself through yesterday. The fact that I didn't sleep last night didn't help either. I spent all my time staring at Montana. Watching, waiting. Making sure she didn't have another nightmare, and that I was right there, awake, if she did. She looked peaceful though.

"She screamed out the name Andrew last night," I tell Gray.

"Andrew? Okay, I'll update Vinny," he says, already tapping out a message on his phone. "You know I'm not letting you do what you're planning on doing." Gray looks up at me. "We have people for this sort of thing, Luke. I'm not letting some prick ruin your life."

"I don't care if it ruins me. I need to find that fucker. I need to do it," I repeat.

"I get that, but I'm not letting you get your hands dirty when the result is going to be the same anyway," Gray says.

"I agree with him. You won't be any good to her if you're behind bars."

I narrow my glare at King, who took it upon himself to butt into our conversation. "I don't recall asking for your opinion."

"You're right. You didn't. I gave that shit to you for free." The fucker smirks.

I roll my eyes and push up from the bench. "I'm assuming you're coming with me."

"Why would I do that?" King asks.

"Because your wife's hanging out at my place today." I raise my brows at him, honestly shocked that he doesn't know where she is for once. Those two are usually joined at the hip.

"I knew that," he grunts, but we all know he's lying out of his ass right now.

"Right, sure ya did." I turn and walk out with Gray and King hot on my heels.

"I have to go get Graycee. I'll catch up with you guys later," Gray calls after us.

"Give her a hug from me," I tell him.

"And tell my girl that her favorite uncle has another puck for her shelf," King adds, as Gray grumbles under his breath.

The moment I shift the car into park, I jump out and walk inside. There's no sign of Montana or Aliyah anywhere. I make my way through to the kitchen, then the living room.

"They're in the theater," King says while waving his phone at me.

I head that way and find Montana curled up on one of the oversized recliners, Aliyah filling the one right next to her.

I reach out a hand to stop King when he goes to walk past me, remembering how Montana reacted to seeing Grayson in the back of the car yesterday. "Wait by the door. I'll let her know you're here first," I tell him, keeping my voice low. King nods as I walk down the few steps before stopping in front of Aliyah. "Your husband's here. You should take him home before he eats everything in my pantry."

Montana jolts and her body stiffens, but she doesn't move her head to look around. She keeps her gaze focused on the screen.

"Right, well, it's been great hanging out with you, Montana. Maybe we can do it again sometime?" Aliyah smiles as she pushes up from the chair.

"Um, thank you." Montana smiles back at her.

"Thanks, Lia." I pull Aliyah in for a hug, drop my arms, and watch her walk away.

"Anytime," she says.

I fill the seat that Aliyah just vacated and reach for Montana's hand, entwining my fingers with hers. "How's your morning been? Lia can be a bit chatty." I chuckle.

"She's nice. I like her," Montana says, though she's yet to look at me.

"That's good. What have you been up to?" I ask as my thumb rubs small circles along the top of her hand.

Montana glances at our joined palms before refocusing on the screen. "Nothing really. We just watched movies."

"Have you eaten?"

"I had some of the fruit you left," she says, then quickly adds, "Thank you."

"That's it?" I look her over. The girl really does need to eat. She's skinnier than I've ever seen her.

"It was enough."

"I'll make you something else. What do you feel like having? Or we can order some takeout?" I offer.

She shakes her head. "No, thank you. I'm not hungry."

"Montana, do you... do you think you should talk to someone? Like a professional? A doctor? I can find someone willing to come to the house."

"Why would I need to talk to someone?" This time, she turns her head to look at me.

"Because you've been through a traumatic experience. It's okay to get help."

"I was in a car accident," she whispers.

"Tanna, we both know that's not true." I sigh, and she tugs her hand back.

"It is true."

"Who's Andrew?" I ask, and the moment the words leave my mouth, I wish I could take them back.

Montana's face goes ashen. Her hands tremble and her body curls in on itself. "W-who?" she stammers out.

"You screamed his name last night, Tanna. In your sleep. So who is he?" I ask again. Because, well, the cat's out of the bag now.

"No one." She shakes her head from side to side. "I should go."

"You're not going anywhere. You need to let me help you. Why are you punishing yourself?"

"I'm not... I... You wouldn't understand."

"You're right. I probably wouldn't. Because the Montana I used to know knew her worth and would never have let some asshole beat her black and blue." I take a deep breath. I need to calm down.

It's not her fault. I know that. I know none of it is that simple. I've looked into it. There's a whole psychology behind domestic violence. Between the abuser and the abused. Some people never make it out on the other side. And the truth is, she's lucky to be alive. I'm lucky she's alive.

But, fuck, why the hell was she letting it happen? She could have come to me.

"The Montana you knew is gone, Luke. She died the day we buried Sean. The same day you walked away from me and never looked back."

"I'm sorry." It's all I can say. "I just... I hate seeing you like this. I hate that you've been going through this alone, and I hate that I didn't fucking know it was happening."

Montana doesn't say anything, so I keep going.

"And you're wrong. The girl I knew is still in there somewhere. I know she is... How's school going? Are you still studying math?" I ask, wanting to change the subject.

"I... I think I'm going to go lie down for a bit, if that's okay."

"You can do whatever you want, Tanna. You don't need permission," I tell her. "Come on, I'll help you up the stairs."

"It's okay. I've got it." She rolls onto her side, then onto her feet, and I watch her walk out of the room. Fuck, I need to find a way to get through to her. I need to help her see what's really going on and how much better she deserves. I just don't fucking know how.

I know she said she'd be okay, but I get up and follow her anyway. Meeting her on the steps. "You didn't answer me about school? Are you still taking classes?" I ask, trying to make light conversation.

Chapter Seven

"I ... I don't..." I choke on my words.

It's a simple question, Montana. He's asking you about school. You should be able to answer him. As I chastise myself, I can feel my heart rate pick up. I'm spiraling out of control.

"Hey, Tanna, it's okay." Luke takes hold of my

arm. "Just breathe. You're okay. You're safe," Luke says, squeezing my hand.

I count to six, out loud, over and over until my breathing returns to normal. I don't know how long it takes, but Luke doesn't move. He stands on the stairs, holding my hand.

"Why six?" he asks when I finally look at him.

"I don't know. I just like the number six." I shrug.

"Out of all the numbers you could choose, *six* is the one that you use to calm yourself."

"It's just a number, Luke." I don't let go of his hand as I continue to make my way up the stairs.

"It's also my jersey number, but you know that."

"It's just a number," I repeat. The fact that the number six seems to be what helps me has nothing to do with him or his jersey.

I'm about to turn and walk into the guest room, but Luke keeps walking, my hand still locked in his as he guides me into his bedroom and then the bathroom. Where he leans across the oversized oval tub, sets the plug into the drain, and turns the faucet on.

"What are you doing?" I ask him.

"Running you a bath. It'll help with the pain," he says, opening the cabinet and pulling out a bag of salts. "I use these after a particularly brutal game. Always does the trick." He pours a generous amount of the salts into the water before grabbing a small bottle of lavender. He adds a few drops of that too.

"You want me to take a bath?" I ask him.

"You soak, relax. I'm going to go make us some lunch."

"I can make lunch. What do you want?" I'm already turning to walk out of the bathroom when Luke stops me.

"*I'll* make lunch. *You* relax." He reaches out an arm, tipping up my chin and forcing me to look at him. "Please, just hop in the bath and enjoy it. Trust me. You'll feel so much better afterwards."

I glance at the tub that's filling up before refocusing on Luke. "You're not staying in here?"

He smirks. "No, I'll be in the kitchen... unless you want me to stay?"

I shake my head while my fingers wring the hem of the sweatshirt.

"Okay." Luke turns around and walks out, leaving me alone. With my thoughts and that tub.

It's just a bath. You can take a bath, Montana.

I give myself a mental pep talk as I close the bathroom door and strip off my clothes. Then I step into the tub and sink down. The water's hot, but it feels good against my sore muscles. I focus on my breathing as my eyes flick around the bathroom. The opulent fixtures and expensive tile work.

I'm in Luke's house. Andrew can't find me here.

I turn off the water, lean back against the tub, and allow my lashes to flutter closed. I will my body to relax as the warmth encompasses me. My mind is whirling. I don't know what I'm doing here. I don't know how long I can stay before *he* starts looking for me. The only thing I do know is that I can't let the mess of my life touch Luke. Because I also don't know what Andrew would do if he found out where I was.

I'm not afraid for myself. He could kill me for all I care. It's Luke I'm worried about. What Andrew might do to Luke, how the drama might affect his career.

Me? I can handle it. I've been handling it for the past three years. Whatever he dishes out as his punishment, I'll survive it. And if not, well, at least my hell will be over with.

I close my eyes and count to six in my head.

Hands clench around my shoulders, pushing me under. I fight to come back up, my body thrashing around the water as I struggle to break the surface. My fingers claw at the arms that are holding me down.

My lungs burn, and as the last bit of fight drains from my body, I'm lifted out and I suck in a lungful of air. Gasping, coughing, and sputtering. "Andrew, please, stop," I beg through strangled breaths.

"I'll stop when I think you're clean enough. You let that filthy piece of shit touch you. You think I'm going to touch you after that? No. You need to get clean," he seethes and pushes my head back under the water.

Again, my body thrashes, the fight for survival taking over as I try with every morsel of energy I have to get up. To suck in some air. Just when I think this is it, that he's not actually going to pull me back up this time, he does.

I don't plead with him anymore. It's useless. If I comply and take the punishment, it'll be over a lot quicker. I should know that he never listens to reason. The truth is I didn't let anyone touch me, but Andrew's convinced I let the server at the coffee shop caress my hand.

"Filthy fucking whore. This is your fault,

Montana. If you just followed the rules, I wouldn't have to do this. But you can't do something that should be so fucking simple, can you?" he hisses at me. "So fucking beautiful, but so fucking stupid." Andrew pauses to cup my cheek, and then he's pushing me back under.

"No!" I scream as my head shoots out of the water, my chest heaving and my own voice echoing off the walls. As my eyes scan the room, the present comes back into focus.

I'm not there. And he's not here.

And then the sobs rack my body. I bring my knees up to my chest, wrapping my arms around them. The bathroom door bursts open, and my body stiffens until I see Luke.

"Fuck, Tanna." He curses under his breath before walking over to the tub.

I don't move. I barely breathe. I can't do anything but sit here and let the tears fall down my face. Luke climbs in behind me, closes his arms around my waist, and pulls me back against his chest.

"I've got you. You're okay," he whispers, his voice breaking, which only makes me cry harder.

I'm not okay. Nothing about me is okay. I don't think I ever will be either.

But right now, I let myself take comfort in Luke's hold as he continues to whisper promises against my ear. Telling me I'm safe, that he's got me.

Eventually the tears dry up and my body starts shaking from the cold instead of the fear. I have no idea how long we sit in the tub. Luke fully clothed. And me, well, *not*. "I'm going to get up and get some towels," he says.

I don't move, keeping my knees drawn up to my chest. I watch him as he pulls his wet shirt over his head and something on his ribs catches my attention. No, not something. A name.

My name. Written in script across his right rib cage. "Luke?"

"Yeah?"

"Why do you have the word *Montana* tattooed on you?" I ask while my mind insists that maybe he just really likes the state...

"It's not a word. It's a name. Your name," he says as he holds out a towel for me to take.

"Why do you have my name on your body?"

"Because I wanted a piece of you with me, in

some way. I knew I couldn't have you, not really, but I could have your name. You were already stamped all over my heart, Tanna, so why not stamp you on my skin?" He shrugs like he hasn't just dropped a giant bombshell.

"I was stamped on your heart?" I haven't moved from the tub. I'm not sure that I can.

"You *are* stamped on my heart, Tanna. You're the only girl I've given it to. You just never knew."

"Why didn't you tell me?"

"Because it's not right. Sean's my best friend. I can't betray his trust."

I nod my head like I understand. But I don't. I don't understand at all.

Instead of asking Luke to explain, though, I take the towel, push to my feet, and step out of the chilled water. I probably should have asked Luke to turn around, give me privacy, because when he gets a good look at my body, a string of expletives falls out of his mouth. His hands fist at his sides and I take a step back. Except there's nowhere to go. My legs hit the edge of the tub as I wrap the towel tighter around me.

"Fuck." Luke runs a hand through his hair before moving towards the door to add more space between us. "I'm sorry. I'd never hurt you, Tanna. I fucking hate that you're scared of me. That I've done anything that made you even a little afraid of me."

"I..." I don't know what to say to that. It's instinct. I can't help the way I react.

"It's okay. The clothes Aliyah bought are all on the bed in your room. I'll be downstairs." He pauses, like he wants to say more. But then he turns, stopping when he's standing on the threshold. "Just know that you will always be safe here. No one is going to lay a hand on you in this house, Tanna."

It's a nice fantasy, but that's all it is. I realized that after the first few times Andrew hurt me, then promised to never let it happen again. And I believed him. I won't make the same mistake twice.

Chapter Eight

Seeing Montana break down the way she did *broke* me nearly as much. I fucking can't wait to get my hands on the fucker who did that to her. The guttural sound of her sobs tore at my heart. I have to find a way to get through to her. She needs help. But before that happens, she has to be willing to admit there's a problem.

Why is she refusing to acknowledge what we both know?

Fuck, her body is covered in bruises. I knew she was beaten badly—looking at her face told me as much. But I had no idea how bad it was until she stepped out of the tub and I saw all the marks on her torso. I've had my fair share of bruises. I'm a fucking hockey player, but that shit that was done to her... I'm surprised she's even up and moving around.

After getting changed, I head downstairs. I pass the living room and an idea comes to mind.

The blanket fort will protect our secrets, Luke. No one can touch them once they're locked in here.

Her innocent childhood words replay in my head. It's worth a shot.

Running back upstairs, I grab a handful of blankets out of the linen closet and drop them in the living room before shifting the furniture into position. Then I go about building the ultimate blanket fort. Once I'm satisfied with my limited architectural abilities, I grab the fur rug from over by the fireplace and set it in the middle. I scatter some pillows around and take one of the throw blankets from the sofa and lay it out. I stand back and admire my handiwork.

Not bad, but it needs something else...

I head into the garage and dig around in a box of Christmas decorations Aliyah made me put up the year I moved in. I find some string lights, head back inside, and drape them around the top of the fort before plugging them in and lighting them up.

Happy with the result, I flick off the room's recessed lighting, close the blinds, and watch the little bulbs twinkle. Then I go into the kitchen and make a quick charcuterie board. I know Montana's not going to eat a full meal, but maybe she'll pick at something smaller. I grab two bottles of water and the wooden board now full of meats, cheeses, crackers, and fruits. And place everything in the middle of the fort. Now, the only thing I'm missing is the girl.

I find Montana in the guest room. She's folding the clothes that are piled high on the bed next to the empty bags. Aliyah likes to shop.

"Hey, come with me for a sec. I wanna show you something." I stand by the door, watching Montana limp from the bed over to one of the dressers.

"I should have put this away. It's a mess. I'm sorry," she says.

"It's not a mess, and you can leave it, Tanna.

Come on, this won't take long." I hold out a hand to her, hoping she'll take it.

"Are you sure?" she asks, her brows drawn down as she stares at the pile in front of her.

"Positive. Come on. I'll help you sort this all out later."

Montana walks over to me, her steps tentative and clearly pained. She's changed into a pair of shorts and a band shirt with her hair piled up on her head. Even covered in bruises, she's still the most beautiful thing I've ever seen. She places her hand in mine and follows me downstairs. I stop on the threshold of the living room and Montana gasps.

"What did you do?" she asks.

"I built us a fort. Come on." I lead her inside and sit down in the middle. Montana sits across from me, her eyes wide and searching. There's a hint of the old Montana behind the pain and sadness I see there.

"You used to annoy Sean and me, asking us over and over again to build these for you when we were kids. You used to love them," I remind her.

"I remember," she says.

"The blanket fort will protect our secrets, Luke. No one can touch them once they're locked in here," I recite her own words back to her.

"That was something said by a child who wanted to believe."

"No. It's true. This fort will protect our secrets, Tanna. And we're going to spill them all. The only people who can hear them are you, me... and the fort."

"I don't know..." she starts, already shaking her head.

I pick up one of the waters, twist off the cap, and hand the bottle to her. "I'll go first." I pull my shirt over my head and point at her name on my ribs. "On the night of Sean's funeral, I went to the tattoo parlor with every intention of getting something to memorialize him. When I sat in the chair, though, that's not what I asked for. I asked for your name. I wanted you to be with me in some small way. I didn't just lose Sean that day. I lost you too, and as much as I hate admitting it, I think losing you hurt more in the end."

Montana stares at me, at her name on my skin. "I... I didn't die, Luke. I was right there. You chose to walk away."

"You're right. I did. And I chose wrong. I never should have walked away from you. I thought I was doing the right thing. By you, by Sean."

Montana sips at the water and then sets the

bottle on the rug. She closes her eyes and opens her mouth. "I... I met Andrew three years ago..."

I reach over and grip her shaky hands. I don't say anything. I just wait for her to continue.

"It was good, during those first few months. I thought I'd found someone who loved me. Who wasn't going to just leave. Everyone always leaves me."

She pauses and a knife stabs right through my chest. I fucking left. I'm part of that *everyone*.

"And Andrew never did leave. He... I don't know what happened, but the change was gradual. Over time, you know. He'd have these sudden outbursts if I did something wrong, or broke one of his rules. I tried to be what he needed. I really did. But I'm just like them, my mom, Sean... I'm too selfish to be any good for anyone else."

I want to stop her. Tell her that's a load of bull-shit. That she's not selfish. She's perfect the way she is. But I bite down on my tongue, too afraid if I stop her now, she won't keep going.

"The first time he hit me, it wasn't that bad. He promised it was an accident and I wanted to believe him. I really thought he would change. Then I would think to myself... *at least he hasn't left me*. If he's stay-ing, then I owe it to him to try harder."

"What happened the other night?"

"I was supposed to drop out of school. I told him that I'd already done it, but I was still studying online whenever he wasn't home. Then I got too preoccupied with one of my exams and forgot to make dinner... And he found my textbooks."

That motherfucker put her in the hospital because she was fucking studying. A red haze clouds my vision, and it takes everything I have to keep my fists from clenching. To keep my ass planted on the floor.

"You know that's not love, right?" I ask her, instead of reacting outwardly.

"I know. But he stayed, Luke. No one else stays," she whispers.

"I'm sorry I left, Tanna. You have no idea how sorry I am," I tell her. "But I promise you I'm never leaving again. I will always be here for you."

She smiles, but I can tell she doesn't believe me. And that's fine. I don't blame her. It just gives me more of a reason to prove it.

"Where is he now? You think he's looking for you?"

Montana shakes her head. "Not yet anyway. He won't look for me until he's sure I've recovered. He always keeps his distance after..."

Her words trail off, and I just want to shout: *After he fucking beats you black and blue?*

"You can't go back there, Tanna. I can have all of your things picked up. I can help you transfer schools but you're staying in Vancouver. If you don't want to live here, with me, I'll get you your own place. But you can't go back."

"I can't ask you to do that for me, Luke. He might not be looking for me now, but if I'm not there when he comes home, he *will* look for me and it'll just be worse."

"No one is getting in this house. You're safe here. And *if* he wants to get to you again, he'll have to come through me first."

"That's exactly what I'm afraid of. I don't want you to get hurt. I don't want this to impact you, your career..."

"It's too late for any of that. Seeing you like this fucking hurts me. Like nothing I've ever felt before. But knowing that I could have prevented it fucking tears me apart, Tanna."

"It's not your fault," she says. I know I didn't do this to her, not directly, but me leaving fucked with her head. That's all on me.

I lie down on the rug, propping my head on one of the cushions. "Come look at the stars with me."

Montana curls up on her side before one of her hands reaches out and grabs hold of mine. "Since we're spilling secrets, I told the girls at school you had crabs your senior year."

"That was you?" I laugh at the memory of being eighteen and trying to figure out why I'd suddenly become girl repellent. "Why?"

"Because I was jealous. I had the biggest crush on you and you didn't see me as anything but a little sister."

"You're wrong. I never saw you as a little sister. I've always been in love with you, Tanna. I've always seen you as the most beautiful girl in the room." I turn my head to face her.

"Not so beautiful right now," she whispers.

"Nothing could ever take away from your beauty."

We lie here staring at each other silently. I want to reach over and kiss her, but I don't.

"When you were in ninth grade and that kid— shit, what was his name...? Hunter Something-or-Other asked you to prom, I threatened to break his knees if he didn't dump you," I admit aloud for the first time to anyone.

"Why?"

"Because I wanted to take you myself." I shrug.

"And I refused to go because I was humiliated after being dumped." She sighs.

Montana fell asleep inside the fort about an hour ago. I picked up the uneaten food and threw it away before I grabbed a beer from the fridge. I had a shit-ton of messages from the guys that I needed to reply to.

Now, I'm sitting on the back porch, wondering how the fuck I'm supposed to help this girl, and what I'm going to do when I have to travel out of town next week. I can't leave Montana here alone. Especially knowing some psycho is out there looking for her. Or will be.

I decide to send Aliyah a message.

ME:

> We have an away game next week. Any chance you can find an excuse to stay at my place? I don't want to leave Montana here alone.

She responds right away.

LIA:

Of course. I'll be there.

ME:

Thank you.

The back door slides open and I pocket my phone when Montana fills the space.

"Hey, you fell asleep," I state the obvious.

"You should have woken me up." She takes a step forward and rubs at her arms. "It's freezing out here. Why are you outside?"

"It's not that cold." I laugh. But stand up, take her hand, and walk into the house before closing the door behind us. "It's time to eat. What do you feel like having?"

"I'm really not that hungry."

"Okay, well, I'm eating, and you're helping me." I lead Montana into the kitchen and sit her on one of the stools. "Watch. I think you'll be amazed by my culinary skills."

Chapter Nine

I wake to an empty bed. It's been the same every day since coming here. I always start off sleeping in the guest room. Then I have a nightmare, and Luke picks me up and puts me in his bed. Where I fall back asleep holding his hand.

He's always gone in the morning. He has hockey

practice every day. He's played two home games too. I didn't go to either, but I have watched him on the huge screen that he has mounted on the wall in the living room. The Knights won both times. I expected Luke to be out celebrating with his teammates, but he surprised me by coming home. Claiming that he'd rather celebrate with me than anyone else.

I don't know how to take his attention at times. I have, however, managed to fall into somewhat of a routine over the last week. As soon as he's finished practice in the mornings, he's here with me. We've talked a lot, he's cooked a lot, and I've tried to pretend like I'm fine. I *want* to be fine. But, on the inside, the truth is I'm waiting for the other shoe to drop. I'm constantly on edge. That feeling of being in the calm before the storm is strong. I don't want to be a doomsayer, but it's hard not to be.

When I walk around this massive house, I wonder why he has such a big place when it's only him who lives here. And how he keeps it so tidy, I have no idea. I'm guessing he has cleaners, but I've never seen any.

After a few more minutes of thinking about things, I finally get up and head straight for the bathroom before beginning my routine of showering, dressing, and making both beds. I look at myself in the mirror, inspecting my now yellowing bruises. I wish I had some makeup, but I don't want to ask Luke to get it for me. He's already spent so much money on buying me clothes.

I don't really know what's happening between Luke and me. *If* anything is happening at all. I feel like I'm getting very mixed signals from him. Other than holding my hand and telling me that he loves me, he hasn't tried anything else. Which I'm grateful for, because I honestly don't think I'm ready. I know I'm not going back to Andrew. What I don't know is where I'm going to go or what I'm going to do... I just need some time to formulate a plan. I need to disappear. Become someone new, so he can't ever find me. Because I know he will look, and I don't think he'll leave me alive when he does.

I caved yesterday and told Luke I'd talk to someone, a professional, in hopes that they can help with the nightmares. I don't know what talking about my problems will achieve, but Luke seems to think it's a great idea. He's arranging to have someone come to the house, so I don't need to leave. I'm not ready to face the public, especially when I still look like I went ten rounds with Rocky.

After I brush my hair and tie it up into a messy bun on top of my head, I make my way downstairs, grab the plate of fruit out of the fridge that Luke leaves me every morning, and go to the theater room. I switch on the Bravo channel and mindlessly watch reality TV. I don't know what else to do to pass the time.

Before I know it, Luke is falling into the seat next to me. "Hey."

"How was practice?" I ask him.

"It was good," he says. "I... ah... I have an away game tomorrow night. I have to leave in the morning."

"Okay." I nod. I know this. "Do you want me to go home?" I don't know where *home* is anymore, but if he wants me out, I'll leave. He's been more than accommodating. It would be selfish to ask for anything more.

"Tanna, this is your home now. I don't want you to leave."

"How long will you be gone?"

"Two days. You could come with me," he offers. "I can get you your own hotel room."

"I don't think I should go with you."

"Okay. Then stay here, and I'll be back before you know it."

Two days is a long time to sit around in this huge house by myself. But that's okay. I can do it. At least I'm safe. No one would think to look for me here.

"I'm going to have a few security guards stationed in the front and back of the house while I'm gone. You might see them walking around. They won't come inside, though," Luke says.

"Why?"

"Because I need to know that you're safe. I need to do whatever I can to protect you, Tanna."

"Where are you getting security guards from?"

"Ah... they work for Gray's family."

My eyes widen. It's no secret what Gray's family does for a living. And I don't mean the part about them owning a hockey team. "Mobsters?" I raise a questioning eyebrow.

"They're good at what they do, and I trust Grayson. He's not going to send over anyone he hasn't vetted."

"They won't come inside?"

"No."

"Okay." I sigh. "I really don't want you to go to so much trouble for me, Luke."

"Tanna, it's not even a little bit of trouble. Besides, I want to look after you. You deserve the fucking world, and I'm going to be the one to give it to you," he says. "But first, I got you something."

"What?"

Reaching into a bag, which I didn't even notice was there by his feet, Luke pulls out a white box with an Apple symbol on it.

"You got me a MacBook?" I ask him.

"I did. But if you don't like this one, we can return it and get something else."

"Why? I mean, it's amazing. But why do I need a computer?"

"So you can keep taking your online classes. I've also set up an account with a bookstore. I want you to order any textbooks you need and have them delivered to the house."

"You want me to study?" I whisper. I'm not supposed to study.

"I want you to do whatever makes you happy, Tanna. I remember how excited you were when you first started taking classes. I remember how much you love math."

"I don't even know if I'm still enrolled. I mean... I think Andrew would have done whatever he could to withdraw me."

"Then we will have your transcripts sent here. Find you somewhere local to go," Luke says it like it's that easy. "Why don't you log in and find out?

Change all of your passwords as soon as you are able."

"Okay. I can do that." I look at the box and then back up at him. "Thank you. I think this is the nicest thing anyone has ever done for me."

Luke smirks. "Then I need to up my game, because it's just a computer, babe."

My heart does a little flip at the endearment. I'm sure it doesn't mean anything. But to me? Well, it does things to me that I don't want to acknowledge right now.

Chapter Ten

I didn't want to leave her. I hate even the thought of not being here for her. There hasn't been a single night she hasn't woken up screaming. I've arranged to have a counselor specializing in domestic violence come out and see Montana at the house. Starting next week.

I know that it's going to take a long time for her to fully recover from this, if she ever does. Three fucking years. She's been living in hell for three fucking years, and I had no idea.

Powering on my phone, I send her a quick message. We're about to take off but I need her to know that even though I'm not there, *I'm still there*. My mind is still on her. With her.

ME:

> Just about to take off. How you feeling?

She replies with a smiley face emoji. Just a smiley face.

ME:

> Tanna? I want you to sleep in my room when I'm not there. I left something on the bed for you.

MONTANA:

> You need to stop buying me things. What did you leave?

ME:

> I'll keep buying you anything I want, but this isn't something I bought. It's just something I thought you'd like to have.

91

MONTANA:

Thank you. Have a safe flight.

ME:

Don't thank me yet. You don't even know what it is. I'll message you when I land.

MONTANA:

Okay.

"You know you look like you're being tortured in the worst possible way," Gray says from where he's seated beside me.

"I feel like I am," I grunt.

"Welcome to the club." King turns to peer over the headrest in front of me.

"What club?" I ask him.

"The *I can't breathe without her* club," Travis says. These away games suck.

I laugh. "Your wife goes wherever we go."

"Yeah, but we don't get to fly together, and she's always bringing one of her cousins along for the ride."

"The Valentinos always travel in pairs," Gray says. "They're a bunch of paranoid fuckers."

Travis glares at him. "That's my family you're talking about, asshole."

"I know. I don't pity you. That's for sure." Gray shrugs.

Grayson has been friends with Travis's wife since the two were kids. Their fathers are business associates. Liliana's family is, well, one of the largest mafia families in the States. While Gray's dominates the Canadian underground.

"It could be worse. You could have my in-laws." King throws a thumb back, gesturing to Gray, who is in fact his brother-in-law.

"Yeah, I'll stick with mine," Travis deadpans.

"Fuckers," Gray mumbles under his breath. He pulls his phone out of his pocket and dials someone before putting them on speaker.

"Gray, don't you have a flight to catch?" Aliyah's voice comes over the line.

"On it, but I have a question for you, Lia. If Liam and I were in a burning building and you could only save one of us, who would you save?" Gray asks her.

All four of us keep our mouths shut, waiting for her answer.

"Easy," she says. "I'd save you." Grayson smirks at King, who looks utterly stricken. "*Because* I know my husband is more than capable of saving himself. He doesn't need me to drag him out of a burning building. He'd drag himself out because if he didn't and he was dumb enough to die on me, then I'd have to remarry. And there's no way Liam King is letting some other guy fuck his wife."

"Damn right," King says.

"Aliyah, that wasn't the question," Gray grumbles.

"Well, you shouldn't ask me to choose between my brother and my husband. Keep in mind, I only have one husband, Grayson Monroe, but I have three brothers, so..." She allows the implication to hang in the air.

"My god, Pops should be training *you* to take over instead of Vinny. You're a hell of a lot more cutthroat."

"Yeah, not a job I want. But thanks for thinking of me. Gotta go. I just got to Luke's place."

"Okay, talk later," Gray says before hanging up the phone.

Liam leans over the seat and smiles at him. "She loves me more than you."

"She didn't say that," Gray grunts.

I reach for my EarPods, plug them in, and turn on a playlist. Tuning out the idiots surrounding me.

The arena is loud. So fucking loud. My head pounds, probably from the lack of sleep. I stayed up all night thinking about Montana. Wondering what she was doing... if she was okay... Fighting with myself for not being able to stop thinking about her. Hating the fact that she's so close and yet so far away at the same time.

I've come to terms with the realization that I'm no longer going to let Sean's ghost come between us. I know he'd be pissed if I started a relationship with his baby sister, but he's going to have to wait until I meet him in hell for him to do anything about it. I should have said something sooner. I should have picked *her* years ago. I never should have let my friendship with her brother stop me from claiming her as mine. If I had, she'd never have gone through the hell she's been forced to endure over the past three days.

"Hey, Vinny just sent this through." Gray flips his phone in my direction, a photo of a guy in his mid-twenties on the screen. "This is your man. Andrew Glenn. He owns a bar called Slime's."

"Who the fuck names a bar *Slime's*?"

"My guess, some slimy-ass motherfucker." Gray shrugs.

"Right." I tap the end of my stick on the ground. We're about to go out on the ice and he's just dropped this on my lap. I can't do a fucking thing about it. I have to play. Although what I really want to do is run out of this arena and get on the first flight home so I can pay this Andrew cocksucker a visit.

"I know you want to go get him. But take that anger out there. Use it to win this game and then we'll swing by your hometown and show 'em what we think about cowards who beat on women."

"Okay." I don't really have any choice but to agree. I mean, I could leave. I'd pay the fine and probably get benched for a few games. But then I'd have to explain to Montana why I didn't play.

I pull my phone out of my bag and send her text.

> ME:
> Are you watching the game?

> MONTANA:
> I am.

> ME:
> Are you wearing my gift?

She sends me back a selfie, and seeing her in my

jersey does something to me. It's almost primal. Like wearing it is the same as marking her as mine.

> ME:
>
> It looks way better on you than it does on me.

> MONTANA:
>
> I'm sure there'll be a thousand puck bunnies waiting for you after the game who would disagree.

> ME:
>
> The only girl I want waiting for me is you.

She reads my message but doesn't send a reply. I might be coming off too strong. But fuck it. I've stayed away and look where that got us. It's time we both stop fighting what was always meant to be. *Us.*

Chapter Eleven

I've read Luke's message more times than I'd ever admit.

The only girl I want waiting for me is you.

What the hell am I supposed to make of that? I don't want to think too much into it and make it a thing that it's more than likely not. I know he's told me he loves me. I get that years ago he might have wanted to be more than friends. But now? I don't think that's the kind of love he still has for me. I mean, how could he? I'm nothing but a broken mess.

I'm not good for him. Hell, I'm not even good for myself right now. I've thought about leaving over and over again over the last two days. I know that if I go back now, I could make things right with Andrew again. He's probably not looking for me yet, which means he wouldn't know that I'm not home.

I also know that if I go back, the cycle is never going to end. I can't fix him. I can't help him. I don't even know if I want to anymore. What I do know is that I'm tired. I'm over being scared of my own shadow, but I don't know how else to be.

When I logged in to my online profile and saw that I was still enrolled in my classes, I did what Luke suggested and changed all of my passwords, including those for my emails and social accounts. Not that I post, ever. I use them for stalking purposes only. Following Luke has been one of my guilty pleasures.

I don't want to go back. That's the conclusion I've come to. It's not that I ever really *wanted* to go back in the first place. I just didn't have other options. And I was too afraid to leave. I still am. I have no idea what Andrew is going to do once he realizes I'm not home and have no intention of returning.

I should let Luke send people to pack up my things. The only reason I haven't is my reluctance to get him any more involved in my mess. I wouldn't be able to forgive myself if something happened to him because he was trying to help me.

"Penny for your thoughts?" Aliyah asks, while nudging my shoulder.

"Huh?"

"You're off either fantasizing about something or someone... *or* plotting the demise of the world? Which is it?" She plucks the bottle of wine from the table and refills both of our glasses.

"Oh, um, I don't know."

"You know I'm not going to pry, and I won't ever ask you to tell me your story if you don't want to tell it. But, if you do want to talk about anything, I'm here to listen. Without judgment," Aliyah says, watching me carefully, as if she's afraid I might run off in the opposite direction.

"Thank you. I do appreciate the fact you haven't asked. I mean, it's kind of obvious." I gesture to my face. "But I, um, I don't think I want to talk about it."

"Then we won't. We'll drink while watching our men skate around on a giant block of ice and knock into each other. Fifty bucks says my brother will get into a fight with someone within the first period." She laughs.

"He does like to throw gloves." I smile.

"Oh my god, you're one of them, aren't you?" Aliyah points at me. "You're an actual hockey fan."

"I... ah... I watch the highlights mostly." I shrug a shoulder. "I used to go to the games. When Sean and Luke played in high school and college, I went to all their games."

"Did you wear Luke's number then too?" Aliyah waggles her eyebrows up and down.

"No." I shake my head. "My brother would have thrown a fit and tore it off me." I laugh. "He was overprotective like that."

"What happened to him? Luke never talks about it. Just mentioned that he passed."

"He... um..." I look down at Aliyah's wrist and spot the long scar that runs along her skin. I don't know if talking about what Sean did is good for her.

She follows my line of sight and offers me a tight smile. "I didn't do this to myself," she says, tracing a finger along the jagged scar. "My mother did. She had some... issues. Mostly with me."

"I'm so sorry." I take a deep breath. "My brother *did* do it to himself. We didn't even know he was struggling. It was just like one day he was here, and the next he wasn't. He left us."

"I'm sorry. That's really shitty."

"It is." I grab the wineglass and down the contents. I don't really ever talk about Sean. I've talked about him more this past week than I have in the last four years. It's easier to lock that pain away, somewhere deep, and not let it out.

"Oh, here they come!" Aliyah squeals, drawing my attention to the television screen.

"Are you a hockey fan too?"

"I'm a Liam King fan," she says, waving her left hand and showing off the huge shiny rock on her finger. "I actually don't like skating. I have a fear of blades and blood."

"And you own a hockey team?"

"My *dad* owns a hockey team. I just own one of his players." She gestures to the screen again.

As the Knights skate out onto the ice, an excitement I haven't felt in a long time builds within me. It could be the wine, but I think it has more to do with watching Luke play. I had Sean convinced I went to his games to watch him and to be the supportive sister I was. Really, I just wanted to see Luke. He moves on the ice with such a strange mixture of grace and brutality. It's mesmerizing.

"I love that we can watch the whole game," I say.

"Why didn't you watch whole games?" Aliyah asks.

"I wasn't allowed." I admit before quickly slamming my mouth shut. "I... ah... I didn't... I..."

"It's okay. You don't need to explain anything to me, Montana." She holds up the bottle, hovering the tip over my glass. "More wine?"

I nod my head, thankful for her understanding and the fact that she doesn't pry. I grab my full glass and raise it to my lips again.

"You'll have to come to a game at The Castle. They're epic. The crowd really comes out for our guys."

"Maybe." I shrug, refusing to commit to anything.

As the game plays out on the screen in front of us, I realize that something's most definitely wrong with Luke. He always plays hard, but tonight he seems off. He's being a lot more vicious. Rougher. He's been pulled off two guys already, and Grayson doesn't appear to want to leave his side.

"Something's wrong," I say aloud this time.

"Yep. I agree." Aliyah picks up her phone. I want to ask her who she's calling but I also don't want to be rude. "Dad, what's up with Jameson?" she questions as soon as the person on the other end answers.

I don't hear Mr. Monroe's response. Aliyah just nods her head.

"Well, tell him that he's making his girl worry. So clean it up," she says and then hangs up.

"Oh my god. No! I don't want to cause trouble for Luke," I tell her.

"That's not causing trouble—trust me. Luke's position on the Knights is locked in."

"I'm also not his girl," I attempt to clarify.

"Yeah, you are. You do know he has your name inked on his body, right?"

"We're friends."

"Yeah, 'cause I go around and get tattoos for all my *friends*." Aliyah laughs.

"It's not like that." I can feel my face heating up.

"But you want it to be *like that*, don't you?" She raises a perfectly manicured brow in challenge.

"I... I'm not in the right headspace to start a relationship with anyone," I tell her instead of answering.

"I know a lot of people would tell you to take

your time, heal yourself, make sure your brain is right and cleared of all that bullshit... But if Luke makes you happy, don't deny yourself because of what anyone else says or thinks. Because of what society tells you is the standard. You do what feels right for you."

"I'm not sure I can trust my feelings right now..."

Chapter Twelve

I look at the time on my phone as my head hits my pillow. It's late and the last message I got from Montana was over an hour ago. I want to call her. I need to hear her voice.

Finding her number in my contacts, I start typing

out a message to see if she's awake when my phone rings and her name pops up on my screen. I hit the accept button and bring the phone to my ear. "Hey, I was just about to text you."

She doesn't say anything, but I can hear her crying. It's not loud but I can tell. "Tanna, what's wrong?" I sit up on the bed.

"I... I just wanted to hear your voice. I'm sorry."

"You can call me anytime, Montana, always. What happened?" I try again. "Is Aliyah still there?"

"Yeah, she's asleep in the other room."

"Okay." *Shit, what the fuck do I say?*

"I'm scared."

"No one is getting inside that house, Tanna. I promise you."

"That's not why I'm scared. I'm afraid of going to sleep," she admits. "Every time I do, I see him. I don't want to wake up screaming with Aliyah in the other room. What if she hears me?"

"Did you not sleep last night?" I ask. This is the second night I've been away.

"No. I couldn't..."

"I have an idea. Plug your phone into a charger. I'm going to call you on video," I tell her.

"Okay."

"Be right back." I cut the call and hit the video chat icon. Montana answers and her face comes into view. "Fuck, babe, how long have you been crying? Why didn't you call me sooner?"

Her eyes are red and raw. "I didn't want to bother you."

"You are never a bother." I set the phone up on the bedside table and lie on my side, facing the screen. "Put your phone next to you."

Montana mirrors my movements, her phone on the nightstand and her head on the pillow.

"We're going to go to sleep together, just like this. If you have a nightmare, I'll hear you," I tell her.

"I'm sorry," she says.

"Don't be. I like sleeping with you."

"I don't want to go back," Montana whispers. Her voice is so quiet.

"You're never going back, Tanna." The thought of her going back to that asshole sends a spark of rage running through me.

"I'm not really sure what I'm supposed to do. I don't have anything, Luke. No job, no savings. Nothing."

"You don't need any of that. I have more than enough for both of us. Whatever you need, Tanna, you can have it."

She shakes her head. "I don't want to be dependent on anyone else. I know I need to get a job. I need to get an apartment. But maybe not when I look like this." She points to her face.

"If you want a job, then get one, but don't do it if you don't really want to." I stop and think about what she said. Her claim that she has nothing. "Tanna, when was the last time you saw your dad?" I ask her.

He wasn't really Father of the Year material, but he wasn't the worst either. He was also pretty well off. I find it hard to believe that he'd turn his back on his daughter, leave her with nothing. Surely if he knew what was happening to her, he would have stepped in, right?

"I haven't seen him for two years," Montana says. "I... Andrew didn't like me seeing him."

"And what? Your dad was okay with that? Just accepted it?" I ask her.

"Not at first, no. I said some pretty hurtful things to him, though. I made sure he would stop calling me."

"He's your father. It shouldn't matter. He never should have stopped," I grunt. She truly was alone, all these years.

"It's okay. I'll get a job and go to school. I can do that, right?"

"You can do anything you want. No one is ever going to stop you from doing anything, Tanna."

"Thank you." She yawns.

"Close your eyes, babe. Go to sleep. I'll be right here."

"Night, Luke."

As soon as I wake up the next morning, I check my phone. Tanna is still asleep. I didn't hear her call out last night, which I'm hoping means she didn't have a nightmare. I pull the charger cord from the bottom, pick up my phone, and take it into the bathroom with me. I don't want to disturb her, but I want to make sure I'm here when she finally opens her eyes.

I take the world's quickest shower, and it's when I'm drying off that Montana wakes up. "Um... Wow." Her voice comes out of the phone's speaker, and I turn around to see her staring back at me. Her eyes widen, and she gasps and covers her face.

"Shit. Sorry." I wrap the towel around my waist, only just realizing I gave her a show. "You can open your eyes now, babe."

"Hey." She smiles at me.

"How'd you sleep?"

"Surprisingly well. Thank you for last night."

"You're welcome. I... ah... I have to make a stop before I come home but I'll be there later tonight."

"Okay, well, I'll let you go and get dressed."

"Talk to you soon." I hang up and walk back into the bedroom, throwing on the suit the team expects you to wear while transiting to and from the games. Then I pack everything up and text Gray to let him know I'll meet him in the lobby.

By the time I get there, it's not just Gray waiting for me. King, O'Neil, and Liliana along with her brother Alessandro are all there too.

"Did I miss the memo about a party?" I ask with a raised brow.

"Yep, we're going on a road trip to your hometown, bro. I heard there's popcorn and a free flight, so I'm in." King smirks.

"You all really don't need to tag along."

"Yes, we do. You're not doing this on your own. Besides, I'm torturing my brother by making him stay in Canada a day longer," Liliana says.

"Okay, let's get out of here." I look at Gray. "What'd you tell your old man?" We're supposed to fly home with the team, and going our own way isn't usually accepted.

"The truth." He shrugs. "Come on. Let's go pay this asshole a friendly little visit."

My fingers tap along the top of my thigh. "Think this car can go any faster?"

"Sure, if you want to end up wrapped around one of these pine trees, instead of actually getting to where we're going. If I die, Aliyah will kill me." King, who is currently sitting behind the driver's seat, looks back at me with a satisfied smirk on his face. "And then she'll kill you."

"You can't be killed if you're already dead, moron." I roll my eyes at him.

"It's Aliyah. You think she wouldn't find a way to bring us all back just so she could kill us again herself?"

"No, she doesn't like the sight of blood. My sister's not killing anyone," Gray chimes in. "Well, not with her hands. She would, however, put you in a coffin full of venomous spiders."

King visibly squirms in his seat. "That's just cruel."

"If you wanted me to be nice, you shouldn't have married my sister," Gray counters.

When the car finally pulls onto the main street, I jump out and walk a block up, stopping when I get to the front of Slime's. A closed, boarded up Slime's. "What the fuck?"

"Looks like our man's on the run," Gray says, pointing out the obvious.

I walk up to the glass door and yank on the handle, surprised when it opens without much force. "Who boards up windows and doesn't lock a door?" I turn to Gray with a raised brow as I step over the threshold.

"A fucking idiot," he replies before following me inside.

I glance around at the dilapidated bar. Every piece of furniture has been smashed and glass covers the wooden flooring along with the alcohol that once filled the bottles.

"Huh." I turn at the sound of Alessandro's voice, Travis and Liliana standing next to him.

"What *huh*?" I ask him.

"Either your man's got some serious anger issues, or you're not the only one after him."

"Come on, let's get out of here. We'll stop by the apartment the asshole had your girl holed up in. If he ain't here, my bet is we'll find him there." Gray clasps a hand on my shoulder before walking out the door.

Chapter Thirteen

Aliyah left thirty minutes ago. She's spent the last two days here. I know that Luke must have asked her to stay, but I appreciate the fact that she did. I haven't had a friend for a really long time. I pushed everyone away, distanced myself. I let Andrew convince me that they weren't my friends. That they were trying to come between us. Now that I think about it, I should have listened to them. Because they were right. He wasn't good for me.

There's still this deep-seated fear that he's going to come and find me. That he's not going to just let me go. I know Andrew. He's not the type to just let things go.

I walk into the bathroom and eye the tub. I'd love nothing more than to soak in a hot bath. But I can't. I know the moment I try, the memories of Andrew holding me under will overtake me. My chest gets heavy at the thought. So I reach into the shower stall and turn on the water. Luke should be home soon. He said he'd be home later tonight and, honestly, I'm doing everything I can to keep myself busy until he gets here.

I need to get a grip on myself. It's not healthy to lean on him so much. But right now, I need help. And I'm starting to allow myself to admit that I can't do this alone. As much as I want to be able to pick myself up, dust off the bruises—*the memories*—and just start a new life, I can't. Because if it were up to me, I would have gone home after I left the hospital. I would have gone right back to Andrew because the fear of what he's going to do when he finds me is too much to handle alone.

Maybe seeing this doctor tomorrow will be a good thing.

I strip off my clothes, step into the stall, and let the hot water wash over me. I know I'm not the first woman to go through what I have with Andrew. I also know a lot of women never escape.

Is that what I've done? Escaped him?

I'm not sure. I'm hiding. I want to be strong enough to just go out into the world and say a big *fuck you* to anyone and anything that tries to stop me from living how I want to live. And hopefully one day I will be. That day isn't today though.

I turn off the water, grab a towel off the counter, and wrap it around myself. Luke has the softest towels I've ever felt. I wonder where he gets them from. I need to remember to ask him.

My palm wraps around the handle, and then I freeze. The sound of footsteps on the other side of the door has my heart pounding. I slowly back up. It's locked. He can't get in here.

I drop onto the tile floor and bring my knees up to my chest, burying my head against my thighs. I just need to wait. He doesn't know I'm here. He can't find me here. I'm imagining things. I count to six. Three times. And just when I convince myself that there's no one on the other side of the door, there's a loud knock.

"Tanna, you in there?" A familiar voice breaks through the pounding in my head.

"Luke?" I push myself up, my knees still shaking as I make my way to the door and open it.

"You expecting someone else, babe?" His smile drops as his eyes rake over my face. "What's wrong? What happened?" he asks, his glare shooting behind me like he's going to find the answers there.

"N-nothing. I'm fine," I tell him. My heart is slowing down and the fear is seeping away.

"Don't lie to me. What happened?"

"I didn't know it was you. I heard footsteps and I just panicked for a bit. It's not a big deal."

Luke takes a step forward, and it's as if he's moving in slow motion as his arms wrap around me and he pulls me up against his body. "I'm not going to let anyone get to you, Tanna," he says. "I promise."

I let myself sink into his embrace. "How was your flight?" I ask, changing the subject while also trying to distract myself from the fact that I'm in nothing but a towel. Pressed up against the one guy I never could stop dreaming about.

Well, me and probably ninety percent of the

female population. I've seen the headlines. Luke has been named the NHL's most eligible bachelor. Not that I'm surprised. If hockey doesn't work out for him, he could easily make it as a model.

"It was fine," Luke replies, holding me tighter. "You're shivering."

"I know." I tell myself to step back. To move away. But my legs don't follow my mental instructions and decide to stay rooted to the spot.

I'm having feelings in places I have no business having feelings. I told Aliyah I wasn't ready for any kind of relationship, that I couldn't trust myself yet. I know that I love Luke. I always have. But I can't trust that love right now.

"You're okay." Luke presses his lips to the top of my head and I make the mistake of looking up at him, staring into those green eyes of his.

"I will be," I say, trying to believe my own words.

"I'll make sure of it."

My thighs squeeze together. There's this need in my core I'm doing everything in my power to ignore. I'm in denial. I might be attracted to Luke, because I'm not blind. But no way is this attraction going to lead to anything more.

I step back and his arms drop from my waist. My

hands hold my towel in place, my fingers clenching around the fabric.

Luke's head tilts to the side as he assesses me. "You know you can ask me for anything and I'd give it to you."

"I know." I nod my head. I don't think he's talking about the one thing I really need right now though.

"I don't think you do know," he says. "Come here." Luke takes hold of my hand and leads me over to the bed. "I know you don't want to acknowledge it. Fuck, you might not even be ready for this, but I'm not about to leave you wanting, Tanna. For anything."

The undersides of my thighs hit the edge of the bed, and Luke presses on my shoulder lightly, guiding me to sit down. "I don't know... Wait. What?" I peer up at him, confused. And then he drops to his knees in front of me.

"You need a release, Tanna. I can see it. And I'm going to give it to you."

"What?" I whisper as his hands land on my bare thighs. I freeze. This is not happening. I need to stop this.

Luke's lips land on my inner thigh as he presses featherlight kisses over the bruises that are still visible there. "No strings, Tanna. Just let me make you feel good," he says as he spreads my thighs wider.

He never takes his eyes off mine as his mouth moves higher. My breathing picks up, and I can feel the need in my core. I've had this dream. A lot.

"You... you don't have to do this," I huff out while trying to move away.

"Tell me to stop and I will, Tanna, at any point. But don't for one second think that I don't want to do this. I've been dying to taste you since I was sixteen."

I stop moving. I don't know what to say, so I don't say anything at all. I look down and watch as his lips continue to move higher and higher. When his tongue finally slides through my folds, all rational thoughts leave my head. The only thing I can think about is how much I want him to do that again.

"Fuck," Luke growls before his tongue slides up the length of my lips for a second time. "So fucking good."

"Oh god." My eyes close and my thighs shake as he seals his lips around my clit and sucks.

Luke pulls away. "Open your eyes. I need you to see me, Tanna. I need you to know it's me."

"It's always you," I tell him. Even when it wasn't him, I would imagine it was. Dream that it was.

I keep my attention focused on him as he returns to the task at hand. It doesn't take long before I climb that mountain, about to soar off the edge. My whole body shakes, and Luke holds my thighs apart when they try to close around him.

"Come for me, Tanna. I want to see it. I need to see it."

Like a button's been pressed, I do come. Harder than I ever remember coming apart before. My hands curl into the blankets beside me and my body seizes up as pleasure like I've never known erupts through my entire being.

Chapter Fourteen

Montana has always been the most beautiful thing I've ever seen, but no image of her I've locked away in my memory compares to the one I'm seeing right now. Her coming apart on my tongue.

Fuck.

I was close to losing all my control. My cock strains in my pants, begging to be freed, as I continue to lick Montana's pussy until every ounce of pleasure has been wrung from her body. Only moving away when I know she's come down from her high.

"That was... fucking amazing." I reach up to cup her face and press my lips to her forehead. "Thank you."

"I'm pretty sure I should be thanking you," she says, a hint of shyness in her voice.

"Trust me, babe, the pleasure was all mine." I look into her eyes. "You good?"

She nods her head while giving me a small smile.

"Okay, I'm gonna hit the shower." I push up to my feet, heading towards the bathroom when she stops me.

"Wait! Don't you want me to..." Montana looks down at my crotch, and I swear my cock jolts at the thought of her touching it... her lips wrapped around it...

"No strings, Tanna. That was for you, not me. Although I thoroughly enjoyed every second of tasting you."

"Um..."

"There are no expectations here, Tanna. I did that because I've wanted to do it for a really fucking long time and because I know you needed it. I'm good. Trust me," I tell her, then walk into the bathroom and close the door behind me. I turn on the cold water, not bothering with the hot. I can see a lot of cold-ass showers in my very near future.

By the time I walk back into the bedroom, Montana is nowhere to be seen. I quickly throw on a pair of sweats and go in search of her. I hope I didn't push her too soon. I could tell she was turned on. Fuck, I wanted to give her that release more than I wanted my next breath.

But what if she wasn't ready for it?

I'm in uncharted waters here and I have no idea what the right thing to do is. I want to do whatever I can to help her, but I also don't want to just fall into that friend zone ever again. I was an idiot to keep us like that all those years ago.

I find Montana in the guest room, sitting on the bed. "Hey." I stay in the doorway. I don't want to crowd her.

"Hey."

"You okay? I'm sorry if I pushed you too far." I run a hand through my wet hair. "I just..."

"It's okay."

"Then what's going on in that head of yours?" I ask her.

"I don't know what I'm supposed to do." She shrugs. "For so long, I've had rules. I've had no choice but to follow those rules. And now... I don't know what I'm supposed to do."

"I already told you. You do whatever you want to do, Tanna. You make your own rules. You make your own expectations."

"What do you want?"

"A lot of things, but what I don't want is for you to do something because you think I want you to do it."

"I'm so broken, Luke. I don't know what I want." She sighs.

"Yes, you do. You've always known what you've wanted, Tanna. You just have to reach out and take it. Everything you've always wanted is right at your fingertips but it's up to you to take charge of your life and take it all."

"I'm scared... I'm not sure I'm ready for everything I want," she admits.

I walk into the room and climb onto the bed, picking up her hand and entwining our fingers. "You don't have to make any life-changing moves right now. You have all the time in the world."

"What if what I want isn't available when I think I'm ready to grab hold of it?" she says, looking across at me.

"Tanna, I've waited ten years for you. I'm always going to be here when you decide you're ready. Hell, I'll wait a lifetime if I have to, because there will never be anyone else for me but you." I can only hope we're talking about the same thing here.

Montana smiles. "Ten years ago, I was thirteen."

"I know."

"I never knew that you noticed me."

"I've always noticed you. You're hard *not* to notice. I just didn't want to admit to myself that I wanted my best friend's little sister."

"And now?"

"Now I'm admitting it. And I'm going to wait, Tanna. You don't need to rush into anything you're not ready for."

"I think I need to get better. I need to sort my head out. I don't think I can be everything you deserve when I'm still stuck in a nightmare half the time."

"I don't need you to be anything but yourself,

Tanna. But I agree. I think you need to heal. I think you need to find yourself again. For you. Not for me. And I'm going to be right here alongside you when you do."

"What if he finds me instead?"

"He'll have to get through me first," I tell her before glancing around the room. "You want to sleep in here or come to my bed?"

Montana chews on her bottom lip. "Your room."

"Come on, let's go." I push off the bed and hold out my hand. Montana places her palm in mine and I lead her into my bedroom. Pulling the covers back before we both climb on and lie down. Then I lean in and press my lips to her forehead. "Night, babe."

I close my eyes and take hold of her hand. As much as I want to wrap my arms around her and pull her up tight against me, I don't.

The shrill scream has me jolting upwards. I flick the light on to find Montana thrashing around the bed. She's screaming out the words "help" and "stop" over and over again. And my heart fucking rips apart at the sound.

I'm going to fucking kill him. As soon as I find the fucker. That's if someone hasn't beaten me to it already. From the looks of his bar and the apartment he shared with Montana, either Andrew was looking for something, or someone else was looking for him.

I haven't told Montana yet. I mean, how do I tell her that everything she had was destroyed? I know I need to mention it to her. Find out if she knows who could be after Andrew and if she could be implicated in anything that he might be involved in.

Gray's brother is looking into Andrew for us, but I need answers. I need to erase him from this world. I'll do anything to make Montana feel safe again.

"Tanna, wake up. It's just a dream," I tell her as I pick her up and sit her on top of me.

Her fingers curl into my arms as her eyes slowly blink open. I fucking hate this, seeing her like this. The fear, the tears that run down her cheeks. I've never felt more useless. I can't take away her nightmares. No matter how much I want to.

"It's okay. I've got you. You're safe here."

"Luke?" she asks as her eyes dart around the room before they meet mine again. "I'm sorry." Her head drops onto my chest and her body heaves with the force of her sobs.

I rub my hands up and down her back. "It's okay. I've got you," I repeat over and over.

She keeps apologizing, but it should be me. I'm the one that should be apologizing for letting her go four years ago. I should have been there to protect her. I'll never forgive myself for walking away...

Chapter Fifteen

Nervous doesn't even begin to describe how I'm feeling right now. My knee bounces up and down as I chew on my fingernail. This was a bad idea. I told Luke I wanted this. That I need this. But now that I'm sitting face-to-face with the therapist he found, I'm not so sure I'm ready for it.

"You're nervous." Dr. West doesn't take her eyes off me. It's not a question; it's a statement, so I don't respond. "You don't need to be. We're not going to do anything you don't want to do. We won't discuss anything you don't want to discuss," she says. "How about we start with you telling me a little about Luke?"

"Luke? Why?" I ask, confused. Luke has nothing to do with why I can't stop the nightmares. Why I have a fear so deep inside me I can't bear the thought of walking out of this house.

"What is your first memory of Luke?"

"I've known him since I was born. Our mothers were friends," I tell her.

"That's not what I asked. I asked you what your first memory of him was."

I think back for a moment. "I believe I was four... or maybe five." I take a deep breath and try to picture that day. "I begged my brother to push me on the swings. Sean didn't want to, because he wanted to climb the fort. Luke stayed behind and pushed me." I smile. There are a million other memories I have of Luke doing little things to make me happy. And then there's the day of Sean's funeral. When he walked out and never looked back.

"Okay, that's good. Do you feel safe here? In this house? With Luke?"

"Yes," I answer, because even if he left when I needed him the most, I know he'd never physically hurt me. I also know deep down if I picked up the phone and called him, Luke would have come for me.

"How did you meet Andrew?"

I jolt at the name. I never mentioned it to her. Luke must have. "I... I met him at a bar he owned." My heart starts pounding. And my fingernails, or what's left of them, dig crescents into my palms.

Dr. West sits across from me, observing my every move. I can feel her eyes on me. "Does talking about Andrew scare you?"

"I don't want to remember," I whisper.

"No one can erase your memories, Montana. What we can do is talk about them. Work through them and find a way for you to make peace with them."

"Make peace with them? I was assaulted for three years, over and over again. I was alone. I had no one but the man who hurt me. But at least he loved me enough to stay. He was the only one who didn't leave, so I stayed too. I don't need a degree to tell me how fucked up I am. So fucked up I'm willing to stay in an abusive relationship just so I could feel wanted. Loved. By someone!" I yell at her, pushing to my feet and running out of the room as soon as the words are out of my mouth.

I can't do this. It was a mistake. I never should have agreed to it.

I run upstairs and into the guest room, closing the door behind me. I go into the bathroom. My fingers grip the edge of the basin as I stare at my reflection. The bruises are fading. In a few more weeks, they'll be gone. All the physical reminders of Andrew will be gone.

But the mental ones... they're not going anywhere. Even now when I'm supposed to be free of him, he still has a chokehold on me.

"I hate you!" I scream as I pick up the marble toothbrush holder and throw it at the mirror, flinching when the glass shatters and shards fall down around me.

I look down at the little pieces before plucking one up between my fingertips. It would be so easy. Sean did it. I could do it too. I could just end everything now, go see my brother again.

The door opens and my head lifts, my gaze meeting Luke's in the broken reflection.

It's ironic. My reflection being broken like this. It's as if it's showing my true self. A broken woman. Lost, confused, angry, scared. I'm all of those things. The one thing I'm not is happy. I don't even remember the last time I felt truly happy.

Luke's glare flicks to the shard in my hand, and his face turns ashen. "Tanna, no," he croaks out as he shakes his head from side to side.

I don't move. I can't. I'm frozen to the spot, caught in a trap of wanting to break free and wanting to just give up. Luke takes slow steps towards me, removes the glass from my hand, and tosses it aside.

"Don't you dare fucking do that to me," he whispers. "Don't leave me. I just got you back."

"No, you didn't. I'm not the girl you used to know, Luke. I'm... broken," I tell him.

"No, you're not. I know exactly who you are, Montana, and broken is not it." He picks me up and walks out of the bathroom. Out of the guest room and into his room.

Sitting on the bed, he positions me so I'm straddling his lap. I don't fight to move off him. Honestly, I don't want to. The only time I feel safe is when I'm with him, and I'll take any reprieve from the fear I can get.

"Who am I?" I ask him, needing to know.

"You're a fighter. You are the strongest person I know. You are a survivor. You are the kindest person I've ever met. You're my best friend, a sister, a daughter. And you're smart, so fucking smart, Montana. I don't know anyone smarter than you." Luke's hands cup my cheeks. "You're mine, and I'm not going to let anyone hurt you again. Not even yourself," he says. "I'm not going to be able to make it up to you, not after leaving four years ago, but I'm going to try anyway. I can't do that if you're not here. I need you, Tanna. I need you to be the fighter I know you can be. Because this? It's a moment in time and we're going to get through it. Together."

His thumbs wipe the tears from my cheeks. "What if I can't fight anymore?" I ask him.

"Then I'll fight for both of us. I love you, Montana. I've always loved you and I'm going to make sure you get your life back."

I shake my head. "My problems shouldn't become yours. You wouldn't even know if your mom never called you."

"You should have called me, the first time. *You*

should have told me, and I would have dropped everything to come to you."

"I know you would have," I admit.

"Why didn't you call?"

My lips press tight together. I thought about calling him once. I even had his number dialed, and Andrew found me. He smashed my phone, and then broke two of my fingers on my right hand. He said that if I ever attempted to reach out to Luke again, he'd break the rest of them and then he'd make sure Luke wouldn't be an issue between us. The veiled threat was enough to keep me away.

"I tried to once." I sigh. "And he... he said he would kill you if I tried to reach out to you again."

"I'd love for him to come and tell me that himself," Luke hisses the challenge through gritted teeth, his jaw clenched and his glare laser-focused.

I flinch and inch off him, scooting backwards onto the bed.

"Fuck, Tanna. I'm sorry." He holds his hands in the air. "I'm sorry. I'm angry. I can't help it. I want to tear that asshole from limb to limb. But no matter how angry I am, I will never take it out on you. I promise."

I nod my head, acknowledging his words. But

they're just words. He's never done anything to make me think otherwise. I know that he's safe. But seeing him so wound up... it just scares me.

Chapter Sixteen

"What are you doing here?" I ask Gray, who is currently standing in my foyer with that permanent pissed-off look on his face.

"Welfare check. You've called in sick for three weeks straight. How much longer do you think the team's going to put up with this self-imposed hiatus of yours, Jameson? 'Cause I gotta be honest. The little pull I actually have with my father is running thin. I've even resorted to using Graycee on the old man, which he totally saw through by the way."

"Let them fire me then." I throw my hands up and walk away. Of course, the asshole follows me into the kitchen.

"Yeah, you and I both know you don't mean that. What's going on?" Gray asks.

"It's my fault." Montana's voice has me turning towards the entryway, where she's standing with her fingers twisting the hem of her shirt.

"No, it's not," I tell her before glancing back at Gray. "I'm on injury leave. If I have to make it long-term, I will."

"That's not happening," he says and then turns his attention to Montana. "You're looking well, Montana. Why don't you stop by the rink, watch a practice, come to a game?" He doesn't bother looking in my direction before he pivots on his heel. "Walk me out, Luke."

I follow him, moving past Montana, who watches us make our way down the long hall. When I reach the front door, I open it and wait. I know whatever Gray has to say, he'll get to it in his own time.

"What's really going on here?" he finally asks me.

"I can't leave," I tell him. "I can't leave her alone." I don't mention why. I don't explain that I'm fucking petrified. Worried that if I leave her alone, I'm going to lose her for good. When I saw her with that piece of glass in her hand a few weeks ago, I freaked the fuck out.

I don't know if she'd actually try to end her own life, but I'm not about to take any chances. Not after Sean. I didn't see it with him. I had no idea what he was planning, that he was struggling to cope with whatever the fuck was haunting him. But I'll be damned if I lose his sister the same way.

Montana might think she doesn't have anything to live for. She's wrong. I'm going to show her that her life can be better. That she can be happy again. I know she's strong enough to overcome this, and until she believes that herself, I'll be right next to her. Reminding her every second of every day.

"What happened?" Gray asks.

"Nothing. Because I'm here. I can't leave. Because if I do and she..." I shake my head. I can't even voice the thoughts in my brain.

"Okay, I'll come up with a solution, because you can't miss any more practices and we need you out on that ice. The team needs you. I need you."

"She needs me more," I tell him.

"I agree, which is why I'm going to figure out a way you can have both." He walks out the door. "And next time I call, fucking answer your phone. It'll save me the trip."

"You live a few houses down. I doubt the commute was bad." I laugh.

"Oh, so you do remember where I live? Good, we're barbecuing tonight. You and Montana are invited," he says. "And before you say no, Graycee wants to see your ugly mug. And I wouldn't recommend disappointing my daughter."

Fucking hell, the dirty bastard has no qualms about using his kid as a weapon against anyone. He knows we'd all do anything for that little girl, which is exactly why he walks away with a smirk on his face. Fucker knows he has me by the balls.

I just have to convince Montana that she can leave the house first. I've been trying all week. Her bruises are all but gone, externally anyway.

"I'm sorry. I can't, Luke. Please don't make me," Montana pleads.

I've been trying to convince her for the last hour that it's a simple barbecue and she can come. That she should come. I know it'd be good for her to get out. She's been holed up in this house for a month. Hasn't even walked outside to the backyard.

I want her to just try. I can't force her, though. Because if I force her to do anything she doesn't want to do, I'd be no better than he is. I refuse to be *him*. I won't take away her ability to make choices for herself.

"Okay, if you really don't want to go, we won't go. We'll stay here," I tell her.

"No, you need to go, Luke. I want you to go see your friends."

"I'm not leaving you alone, Tanna."

"I won't be alone. I've already messaged Aliyah. She's coming over with wine." Montana smiles.

"You messaged Aliyah?"

She nods her head. "I don't need a babysitter. I know why you've been hovering and I appreciate everything you've done. But I'm good. I promise. I have no intention of following in my brother's footsteps, Luke. I wouldn't do that."

I take a deep breath and close my eyes. I don't want to leave her here. We still haven't been able to find Andrew. Although it's not like I've been out there looking for the asshole either. Gray's family is searching for him. And, honestly, if they can't find him, there isn't much of a chance of me doing that shit on my own. The resources the Monroes have are limitless. I'm surprised the guy's gone undetected this long.

"Please, Luke, don't make me the reason you don't see your friends," Montana says.

"You are my friend, my best friend," I tell her.

She looks up towards the ceiling. "Huh, I really thought Sean would strike us down with lightning or something if he ever heard you say something like that." She smiles at me and I swear the room brightens and the heaviness in my chest eases slightly.

"Tanna, I'm serious. I don't care about anyone else. What I care about is you."

She opens her mouth to respond and then the doorbell rings out. "That will be Aliyah," Montana says, jumping up and rushing towards the entryway.

"I hope you don't mind me inviting her over. Shit, I should have asked first. I'm sorry." She glances at me over one shoulder, her eyes wide as she takes a few small steps backwards. Literally and figuratively.

"This is your home now, Tanna. You can invite anyone you want over. You never have to ask me."

"Okay, but still... I'm sorry."

The doorbell sounds out again. "Come on, let's go let Lia in before she huffs and puffs the door down." I hold out my hand to Montana. I can see the indecision, the fear on her face for a split-second before she accepts my offer.

I've been careful to keep things more platonic between us—well, as platonic as I can be, with her. Ever since I saw Montana break down in the bathroom, I haven't pushed her for anything more than the friendship we've always had.

And let's just say... there've been a lot of cold showers. I wake up with her body curled next to mine every morning, and there's that moment between sleep and awareness where I let myself believe that she's mine in every way I want her to be. And she will be. Eventually. I just need to give her time and space to work on herself, so she knows what she wants.

She's been talking to Dr. West every day. Some-

145

times, she'll end the sessions early; others she spends the whole hour talking things out. I'd love to say it's helping, but she's still having nightmares, calling out in her sleep.

I open the door, and Aliyah pushes past me, two bottles of wine in her hands. "I've brought supplies, and we're ordering in. I'm thinking Thai."

"That sounds amazing," Montana says.

"Why are *you* here? Aren't you supposed to be at Gray's?" Aliyah asks me.

"Ah, yeah..." I look to Montana. "I could use a girls' night, though."

"Nope, no way. We have shit to talk about. Shit that's not for your ears. So off you go. But if anyone asks, I'm not here. I told Kathryn and Lil that I was staying home tonight."

"Why?" I ask, a little shocked Aliyah would lie to her two best friends.

"Because I'm not ready to share my new friend with the world. And until we're ready..." Aliyah points between Montana and herself. "...no one needs to know about her."

I have no doubt that Kathryn and Liliana *know* about my new houseguest. Liliana did tag along with us when we went to hunt down Andrew. She didn't know the reason, though. It's not my story to share. It's Montana's. To share, when and if she wants.

"Okay, I'm going. But I'll just be down the road, Tanna. If you need anything, call me," I tell her.

"I'll be okay. Go... See your friends," she says.

I look at her for another minute. I really don't want to fucking leave her.

"Luke, go. I'm sleeping over, so I'll be here all night," Aliyah tells me.

"Okay. But I won't be long." I sigh before walking out the door.

Chapter Seventeen

"I thought he'd never leave," Aliyah huffs.
"Thank you for coming over. And I'm sorry you're missing the barbecue."

"Come on, let's get this party started. And don't be sorry. Gray will probably burn everything he grills anyway." Aliyah walks right past me.

I follow her into the poolroom. I've avoided this place like the plague. I don't do so well with bodies of water. Standing at the doorway, I watch as Aliyah lowers herself onto one of the loungers.

"Well, don't just stand there. Come on in," she says before uncorking a bottle of wine.

"Um.... can we go in the living room or the theater room instead?" I ask her, not moving from the doorway.

"You don't like the pool?"

I shake my head, thankful when she stands up and walks towards me.

"Okay, let's do the living room," she says without pressing for an explanation. That's the thing I like most about Aliyah. She's not pushy and never questions why I can't or won't do something.

"Thank you."

"Pfft, it's your house. You get to decide where we party, Montana."

I don't correct her. Even though we both know this is Luke's house. Not mine. I curl up on one of the sofas and take the glass Aliyah pushes in my direction.

"Do you live close by too?" I've just now realized I haven't asked her much about her life. Other than the fact she's married to Liam King, and that she's

Grayson Monroe's sister, I don't know much about the woman.

"Not too far. Liam didn't want to live this close to my brother. They have this whole love/hate bromance thing going on. Neither one of them wants to admit they actually like each other."

"Is that hard for you?"

"No, because they're both great guys. They love me. And besides, it's fun to watch." She shrugs. "So, what's been going on inside these walls?" She raises her eyebrows.

"Nothing." I sigh. "Luke won't leave. He's afraid I'm going to... Well, he thinks if he's not around, I'm going to do something awful."

"Are you? Going to do something awful?"

I shake my head. "I don't think so. I don't want to be the reason he's not playing."

"What if you come to the rink? I can be there with you. I mean, I don't need an excuse to watch Liam play."

I consider what she's asking. I want to go. I would love to see Luke play, actually be there to watch him. "What if people know?"

"Know what?"

"What happened to me? Why I'm here with Luke?" I ask her.

"No one is going to know anything you don't tell them yourself. Trust me. You're here with Luke because you're childhood friends. That's it," Aliyah says. "There's a game this weekend. Why don't you come and sit in the box with me? It'd just be us girls, me, Kathryn, Lil, and little Graycee."

"I'll think about it."

"What if I pretend that we've never met? The other girls don't know that I've been hanging out here. I don't blab other people's business. It'd just look like Luke's finally decided to stop keeping you to himself."

"In a box? No one else will see me there?" I'm not going to lie. I'm petrified. Thinking the second I walk out of this house, Andrew is going to find me.

"No one will see you. Just us. And it'll be fun."

"Okay." I smile. "I guess I'm coming to my first Knights game."

"First of many." Aliyah lifts her glass and clinks it against mine.

I stare down at the blank page. Dr. West wants me to start journaling. She seems to think it'll help the healing process if I write my thoughts down on paper. The thing is, I don't even know where to start.

I close my eyes. I wanted to do this today. I wanted to try. I'm going to my first game tonight, and Luke is overly excited about the whole thing. I can do this. Though I'm not sure how to start. *Dear diary* seems too childish. So I decide to write to Sean. Thinking that maybe it'll make it feel like I'm actually talking to someone and not just myself.

> Dear Sean,
>
> I may have officially lost my mind. I'm writing to you. My dead brother, knowing full well you'll never read this. Because of what you did. Why? It's the one question I'm probably never going to get an answer to. Why did you leave me?
>
> I guess if you are up there looking down on me, you know what hell my life has been since you've been gone. You also know that I'm now living with Luke. You remember him, right? The best friend you always warned me not to fall in love with. Even though I can't actually remember a time I didn't love him.

I'm trying to get better. I don't want to be this... broken. I want to be the girl I used to be, and if you have any kind of afterlife powers, I could really use your help today. I'm going to a Knights game. I'm leaving the safety of this house. And I'm scared. I don't want to embarrass Luke if I have a panic attack while out in public. I'm also scared that he's out there waiting for me.

Andrew. I can't beat him. This is his game. He makes the rules and he always wins. Maybe this last month has been a reprieve from him, but I know he's going to find me. And when he does, well, it's not going to be pretty.

I've thought about taking self-defense classes. Maybe I can ask Aliyah to take some with me? She's nice. You would have liked her. I think you would have really liked all of Luke's new friends.

I'm not sure what else I'm supposed to write. I'll try again tomorrow. I'll let you know how the game went.

—Montana

"Hey, you ready?" Luke asks. I close the journal

and set it down on the coffee table. He eyes it briefly before landing his glare on me again.

"Yep. Let's do this." I push up from the sofa and make my way over to him.

"You know I will leave the ice to take you home at any point."

"That's not happening. I'll be fine." I try to believe my own words. Even if I'm not fine, I'm not going to do anything that would force Luke to leave mid-game.

"I know you will be, but I want you to know that you come first, Tanna."

"Thank you, but I want to watch you play. It's been years since I've seen you on that ice in person. It'll be fun." I smile at him.

My heart beats wildly in my chest, my hand squeezed tight in Luke's. He's already in his gear. He made me wait with him in a private dressing room. How he managed to arrange that, I have no idea. But the game's about to start and he's walking me up to the Monroe family box.

His hand is still clasped in mine when we push through the door. Luke gives me another reassuring squeeze. My nerves ease a little when I see Aliyah waiting for me.

"Aliyah, this is Montana. Montana, Aliyah," Luke says, as if we've never met. It's a little odd but they both agreed to keep my reason for being in Vancouver under wraps. So she plays along. I have to admit it's somewhat easier, not having to explain that we've met and why. "And this is Kathryn and Liliana," Luke adds, gesturing to the other two women in the room with us. "Montana's going to watch the game up here with you all."

"Great, come on. Let me get you a drink." Aliyah hooks her arm around mine and pulls me towards the minibar.

I glance over my shoulder and smile at Luke. I don't want him to worry about me when he's supposed to be focusing on the game.

Chapter Eighteen

Coach benched me. I can't really say I'm surprised. I've missed three weeks of practice and games. I *am* surprised I haven't received a huge fucking fine. I know I have Gray and his connections (or his father's connections) to thank for that. As far as the world knows, I was recovering from a minor injury and just received clearance to play today.

We're in the second period. I've yet to have any ice time, and I don't think I'm going to. It's okay, though. Sure, it sucks but I'm still here, with my team at The Castle, the Knight's arena. And there's nothing better than a home game crowd, my name being chanted over and over. I know they're all waiting to see if I actually play or not. I think the whole team is. When the second period timer goes off, I know it's not likely.

I walk down the tunnel into the dressing room. I want to reach for my phone. I want to call and check on Montana. I don't do that. Coach doesn't need any more of a reason to be pissed off at me. Instead, I sit on the bench in front of my locker and wait. It doesn't take long for the room to buzz with activity. Every player has their own intermission routine or ritual, depending on who you're looking at.

Right now, Gray is on his phone, stripping out of his gear. He calls his daughter and then spends at least ten minutes in the shower. Travis sits on the bench, his head tipped back and his eyes closed. I can never tell if he's praying or meditating, but that's what he does for the first ten minutes, and God help anyone that tries to talk to him.

King takes a shower and sprawls out on a massage table. He has two PTs working on him at the same time. Me? I usually strip off my skates and jump on the bike or treadmill while I watch reruns of plays on a tablet. I need to keep moving to keep my muscles warm. But since I know I'm not playing tonight, I'm content to sit here and watch everyone else carry on with their business.

Like clockwork, five minutes before the third period starts, Coach gathers the team and goes into his usual pep talk. He runs through plays and then sends us out. I'm halfway down the tunnel, the last player to walk through the door, with Coach right behind me.

"Get ready, Jameson. You're going out on second rotation," he says.

I nod my head. "I'm ready, Coach."

"I fucking hope you are. You've been MIA for three weeks with some mysterious injury that I wasn't made aware of. Whatever the fuck was wrong with you, I hope for your sake and the team's that it's sorted."

I don't tell him that nothing's *sorted*. It's a damn miracle that Montana left the house tonight. I have a feeling if it weren't for Aliyah's encouragement, she might not have.

Aliyah blows up my phone daily, asking if she can come around. I always refer her to Montana—it's her decision if she wants visitors or not. Some days, she doesn't want to see anyone, especially after talking to Dr. West.

Her sleep is still shit, which is evident from the black bags under her eyes. I don't think she'll sleep soundly again until she knows for sure that, that asshole Andrew is six feet under. And I can't wait to be the one to deliver that message to her.

I take my place on the bench and watch the ice. The puck drops and we win possession. Gray and King are right next to me, all of us waiting to get out there and show everyone the line our team's been missing.

The moment we get our chance, I'm jumping over the board and inserting myself in the game. When you've been playing for as long as I have, missing three weeks is nothing; it's almost muscle memory at this point.

Gray steals the puck and the three of us take off down the rink, rushing the net. The Winnipeg Maples are right on us. Their defense is good. I've been watching closely all night, which is why when Gray passes the puck to his right, to me, I fake a left and maneuver around the guy who's been slowing down since the start of the second period.

I see the opening. It's small, but it's there. Right between their goalie's legs. I take my shot and watch as the puck slides through and hits the back of the net. The lights go red, the horns blare, and smoke blasts from the corners of the rink. The crowd screams as a sea of Knights jerseys jumps to their feet. Clapping and cheering.

I drop to a knee with my stick in the air. "Fuck yeah!"

Gray and King slap my back as I look up and see her. Montana is standing in the window. I kiss my glove and raise it towards her. And that's when the cameras decide to hone in on that damn box, plastering Montana's face up on the jumbotron. The moment she notices, her eyes widen and she moves back. Out of view.

"Fuck," I hiss. Then look to Gray.

"Don't even fucking think about it. Come on, I'll call Lia from the bench. They're together. She'll be fine," he says.

I nod my head, not believing for a second that Montana's fine. She's going to try to pretend to be, but I know her. She's scared of being seen and her face was just plastered on that giant screen. Viewed by tens of thousands of people, not to mention how ever many hundreds of thousands are watching the game from their living rooms, pubs, and anywhere in this country that has a television.

I jump over the bench. And before I can storm down the tunnel, Gray slams a hand against my chest, pushing me onto the seat.

"Wait," he grunts. Then he holds out a hand, talking to someone. I don't care enough to look up and see who, before he's dialing a number into a phone.

I don't hear what he says. I don't even hear the noise of the crowd. My gaze is hyperfocused on that window. She needs me. I need to get to her. I can feel it in my bones.

Gray dangles the phone in front of my face. "It's Montana."

I pull off my helmet and snatch the device out of his hand. "Tanna, you okay?"

"I'm okay. That was a great goal, Luke," she replies, her voice quiet.

"We can leave, if you want... If you need to go, we can leave," I tell her.

"No, the game's almost over. What I want is for you to go back out there and score again."

"You sure?"

"Yes, I'm sure. Go and finish the game, Luke. I'll be watching," she tells me.

"Okay." I hang up and pass the phone back to Gray. "Thanks." I nod at him as I slide my helmet back on. If Montana wants to watch me score again, then that's exactly what I'm going to do. "Put us in, Coach!" I yell over the chatter of my teammates.

Coach glares at me, shaking his head before signaling for our line. The minute my skates touch the ice, I'm body-checked into the boards, hard enough that I almost fall back over onto the bench.

"Fucker," I grunt while pushing the huge fucking Maple player off me. I'd love nothing more than to throw gloves. But just as the thought enters my head, Gray is there. Right beside me, his gloves already on the ice and his fist slamming into the asshole's head.

This is what I love about this sport. No, not the fighting, but the being part of a team. Knowing that Gray will always have my back on and off the ice, and I'll always have his too. Which is why, when he gets the fucker on the ground, I help the refs pull him off. My friend is known to be a little hot-headed at times and doesn't always know when to stop.

Chapter Nineteen

Dear Sean,

Last night was bad. Every time I close my eyes, I see him. Andrew. It's as if his hold on me is never going to end. I don't know how to make it stop. If I could just make the images go away, I'd be able to sleep. I'd be able to move on.

I went to Luke's game last night. You would have loved it. I wish you were here to see how successful he is. I pictured you on the ice with him, and then I blinked and you were gone.

Why can't you be here? None of this would be happening if you had just stayed. It's been four years, Sean. I'm supposed to be over losing you. It's been long enough, but right now, I could really use a hug from my big brother. I need you, Sean, and you're not here.

I worry that I'm too much for Luke, that my issues are going to drive him away. Of course, he won't admit that. He seems to think everything will be fine. But it's not fine. It's probably never going to be fine again.

I had my face on the jumbotron last night. Remember when I used to love when that happened? Yeah, not so much anymore. Last night, I wanted to erase it. I wanted to not be there. I'm worried that Andrew somehow saw it. That he's going to know exactly where I am and he's going to come for me. I don't want him to find me. I can't go back to the way things were. I'd rather be with you.

I don't know what to do. I don't even know if writing these letters to you is helping. I'm sitting here, in a corner of some random living room that nobody uses, with tears running down my face.

Until next time,

Montana

I close the journal and swipe at my cheeks. I'm angry that I let myself get this upset. I'm tired and frustrated that I can't just get over it. I want to close the door of that chapter of my life, but it's as if there's a wedge in it. Something keeping it open. I want it to be done. I need it to be done. I'm not strong enough to do this.

I push myself up from the floor and walk out of the little hiding spot I found. I need to wash my face before I let Luke see me. So I make my way into one of the many powder rooms he has in this gigantic house. Turn on the cold water and splash my face. Then I glance up at my reflection in the mirror. I'm starting to look like the old me, the me I was before Andrew. Well, besides the bags under my eyes.

I can do this. I need to do this.

I shut off the water, count to six in my head, and

then go in search of Luke. It doesn't take me long to find him. He's in the kitchen, making lunch.

"I'm starting to think you have a food fetish," I tell him while placing my journal on the counter. Luke eyes the little notebook but doesn't say anything. I'm not worried about him reading it. I know he won't.

"I like to eat. And you need to eat." He points a spatula at me.

"What are you making?"

"Tacos. Everything is already on the table, and this..." He picks up a frying pan and empties the meat into a serving dish. "...is done. So, let's eat."

I follow Luke over to the adjoining dining room and see that the table is full of every ingredient you could possibly imagine for tacos. "This looks amazing."

"Thanks. Now eat up, buttercup." He grins.

"Buttercup?" I raise an eyebrow at him. *That's a new one.*

"I'm trying on some pet names. I'll let you know when I find one that suits you."

"I think Tanna suits me just fine." Luke and Sean are the only ones who ever called me that. Everyone else always called me Montana.

"Okay, we'll stick with Tanna." Luke nods as he

piles up his taco shell. "I have an away game. We're leaving tomorrow."

My heart starts pounding in my chest and I do everything I can to hide my panic. He's leaving again. I know he has to, but that doesn't mean I want him to go. I need him, which isn't his problem. It's mine.

"Okay, I'll be fine," I tell him, not believing for an instant that I will be.

"I'm taking you with me, Tanna. Aliyah and Liliana are coming too," Luke says.

"You want me to come with you?" I set my food down and turn to look at him.

"I always want you with me."

"But why? I mean, won't I just be a distraction? You almost walked out of a game last night because of me, Luke. I don't want to be the reason you throw your career away."

"You are not a distraction, and my career is just fine. I still have a good ten years left, and I'm not spending them leaving you behind."

"Where will we stay?" I ask.

"The team books hotels. They block off the entire floor. There'll be security. But if it makes you feel better, I can arrange for private security too," he says.

"No, you don't have to do that."

"It'll be fun. Our first trip away together."

My brows draw down. "Did you get hit on the head a little hard last night? We've been away together a ton of times. Every summer as kids, if I remember correctly."

"But we weren't dating back then. I didn't get to sleep with you in my arms back then."

"Are we dating?" I'm confused. Luke hasn't even tried to kiss me since that one time he gave me the best orgasm of my life. Actually, come to think of it, he didn't kiss me then either. At least not on my lips...

I can feel myself blushing at the memory.

"Is that what you want? To be dating?" Luke asks, his eyes assessing my face for any sign of... I don't know what.

"I... But we don't... You don't..." I can't get the words out. If he's under the impression that we're dating, why hasn't he tried to kiss me? It just doesn't make sense to me.

"I'm not going to pressure you or do anything you're not ready to do, Tanna. The ball is in your court. When you're ready to take our relationship further, that's when we will. Until then, I'll wait. As long as it takes," he says. "There is no rush."

The ball's in my court.

I jump out of my seat and lean over the corner of the table. Take his face in my hands and do something reckless. Something I've dreamt of doing since I started crushing on my brother's best friend as a kid. I slam my mouth down on his.

Luke recovers from his shock quickly. His hands cup the back of my head and his tongue pushes through my lips, circling around. He groans as he stands, effortlessly picks me up, and sits me on top of the table without breaking the kiss. He steps between my parted legs. My arms snake around his neck.

I want this. I need this. And it's okay to want it.

I've been talking to Dr. West about my attraction to Luke this week. At first, I thought I was leaning on him because I wanted him to help me. It was through talking with Dr. West that I realized that's not true. I've always wanted to be with Luke. This isn't a new feeling. It's just one I'm finally embracing without all the guilt that usually follows it.

Chapter Twenty

Fuck... I can feel the heat of her pussy through her panties, her wet fucking panties. Currently resting against my crotch. I lean closer, pressing myself against her heat. I've been holding back, avoiding being physical with

Montana. I didn't want to rush her. I don't want to be too forward. I can't risk scaring her away. She's starting to settle into a routine here, and I won't do anything that will impact that.

Which is why I pull back, just a little, and break the kiss. "Are you sure about this?" I ask her. "I'm serious, Tanna. We really don't need to rush."

Montana's eyes flick down to where our bodies meet, where my cock is pressed up against her lace-covered pussy. "I'm sure. But if you're not, we can wait."

"Me? This has nothing to do with me being sure, babe. I've wanted this since I was sixteen," I tell her before slamming my lips back down on hers. I groan into her mouth. Everything about her is intoxicating. I want more. I want it all. "Fuck, I need you," I growl between kisses.

Montana responds with a moan. Her head dips back and her chest arches upwards. Her breasts begging me for attention. My hands land under her ass. I pick her up, and she wraps her legs around my waist.

With a few long strides, I walk through the house. I had every intention of taking her upstairs to the bedroom. I want to lay Montana out on the bed, take my time worshiping her the way she deserves to be worshiped. But those plans go out the window when she tightens her legs around me and begins grinding. I swallow her moans, take a left turn, and walk into a living room. This house has a few of them. Why one person needs so many sofas, I have no idea, but I think I just found the perfect use for them.

Fucking Montana in every part of this house.

I spread her out on one of the cushions, my body covering hers. "Tell me what you want?" I rise onto my knees, my fingers hooking into the side of her panties as I pull the material down her legs.

"You," she says.

"Tell me exactly what you want, Tanna. How do you want me? What part of me do you want?" I smirk down at her flushed face.

"You know what I want, Luke."

"I want to hear you say it, Tanna. Tell me," I urge her again, my hands working the buttons on the baby-blue blouse she's wearing, before spreading it wide to reveal her perfect fucking tits wrapped up in a pretty white lace bra.

"I want you inside me. Don't make me wait any longer, please," she says, her voice quiet as her hips rise slightly.

"What part of me do you want inside you, Tanna? You want my fingers?" I ask, and she shakes her head. "My tongue maybe?" She appears to consider this one, and then her head moves from side to side. "My cock?" I lift a curious brow.

She smiles and nods. "Yes, that. I want that."

Unclasping the clip on the front of her bra, my hands then move the material away from her breasts before cupping each one. I stare at them as I massage the flesh around in my palms. "Fuck, these are perfect." I lean down, placing a kiss on top of each. "I can't wait to fuck them," I tell her.

"Luke..." Montana moans.

"Yeah, babe?" I smile while kissing my way up her neck.

"I need you, please."

"You have me."

"I need you to fuck me, Luke. This is torture. Don't make me wait. I've waited so long already."

I sit up slightly and push my shorts down my legs before freeing my cock. My palm wraps around it, stroking a few times. And just as I line the tip up with her entrance, I stop. "Fuck."

"What's wrong?" Montana asks, looking between our bodies.

"I need to get a condom." I move to push off the sofa.

"Or you don't and you can just pull out? Please, Luke, I can't wait." Her legs tighten around my waist, holding me in place.

"You sure?" I've never gone bareback before. I would never risk having a mini-me show up on my doorstep. But right now, that consequence doesn't send me into a panic. Not with Montana.

"I'm sure. I mean, only if you are. I'm clean. I swear."

"I'm not worried about that," I tell her as I slowly sink inside her. My eyes stay connected with Montana's as I fill her up.

She inhales deeply before letting out her breath. "It's..."

"I know," I say while cupping her face with my hand. I was in a frenzied rush to fuck her before. But now that I've entered her, all I want to do is take my time. I want to savor every moment of being inside her. The feeling that's consuming me right now is foreign, something I've never experienced before. "I love you, Tanna." I pull my cock out slowly, then push back in again.

"I love you," she says. "It's always been you."

I cover her lips with mine, and as my tongue

explores her mouth, I make love to her. I try to convey with my movements just how much I feel for her. I don't think it's enough; it'll never be enough.

Her pussy starts to spasm around me and her nails dig into the skin on my back. I continue to slowly fuck her through her orgasm, swallowing her moans. When I feel her body relax, I sit up, pull my cock out of her, and wrap my fist around it. Two pumps and I'm spilling my seed onto her stomach.

"Fucking hell, I think you really were made just for me, Tanna."

"I think we were made for each other," she says.

"I think you're right."

I ordered pizza while Montana was in the shower, the tacos finding a new home in the trash can. It's wasteful, but I'm not feeding her cold or reheated shit. I lay the three boxes out on the table and then get two beers out of the fridge.

Montana walks into the dining room, her wet hair hanging over one shoulder. "You really are the most beautiful woman I've ever seen," I tell her.

"Come eat. I got your top three." I point at the pizzas.

"What happened to the tacos?"

"They went cold." I shrug.

"I could have reheated them. You didn't need to order all this pizza," she says. "It's a lot."

"But I knew you'd like a slice of each: pepperoni, bacon pesto, and pesto mozzarella. They're still your favs, right?" I ask her. I watch as she looks down at the open boxes.

"I'm not allowed to eat pizza."

My brows draw together. "What do you mean you're not allowed to eat pizza?" I move the boxes around and Montana backs away from the table almost like she's afraid the food is literally going to jump up and attack her.

She shakes her head. "I'm not allowed," she repeats, but it's as if she's talking to herself more than me.

"Tanna, it's okay." I stop in front of her and she finally looks up at me. Her eyes glazed over.

"I can't eat pizza."

"Yes, you can. If you want to eat pizza, you can eat it," I tell her.

"No, I'm not allowed. I'll get in trouble. He'll…" She stops herself.

My hands fist at my sides. *That asshole didn't let her eat fucking pizza. Fuck me.*

"Tanna, he's not here. He's never going to hurt you again. I promise. You make your own rules now, remember? It's up to you. Everything is up to you to decide for yourself. If you don't want the pizza, I'll get you something else. But you do need to eat."

She looks at me for a long moment, neither of us saying a word as she processes whatever the fuck is going on in her head. "I can eat the pizza?" She says it more as a question.

I nod my head silently.

"I'm sorry. I just... I don't know how to stop it," she admits.

"Stop what?"

"His voice, in my head. It's always there, reminding me of the rules." She sighs. "The only time it's quiet, the only time he's not there, is when you're touching me."

I reach out and take hold of her hand. "Like this?"

Montana nods and I smile back at her.

"Well, it just so happens that I fucking love touching you, so get used to me being glued to you, babe." I smirk. "Now, do you want to eat pizza? Or do you want something else?"

She appears to debate her decision for a minute before nodding again. "I want to eat the pizza."

I guide Montana back over to the table. "Can you eat one-handed? Because I'm not letting go," I tell her as I take my seat with her hand still firmly in mine. If my touch helps ground her, then I'll be sure to never let go. It's not like it's a hardship.

Chapter Twenty-One

I'm nervous, but I want to do this. The alternative—staying in Luke's big house alone —is less appealing than getting on Aliyah's family jet and flying to Las Vegas to watch the Knights play. I've also never been to Vegas. I haven't really traveled anywhere before.

When I mentioned to Luke that I didn't have my passport, he grabbed a box from his garage and handed it to me. He explained how he went to my apartment the last time he was away and retrieved a few of my things. At first, I freaked out, until he said that there was no sign of Andrew and that the place had been ransacked.

I glanced inside the box and saw the few possessions I actually treasure, along with my passport and birth certificate. But most importantly, Luke found my brother's jersey and the one framed picture I kept of Sean, Luke, and me. It was taken when I was thirteen and I had to hide it in the same box with Sean's jersey. I don't have a lot of things I'm attached to. I left most of my belongings at my father's house.

Thoughts of my dad bring back all the hurtful things I said to him. I know I pushed him away, but he also gave up on me. A parent isn't supposed to give up on their child, or at least that's what I thought. In my experience, that's all parents do though. First my mother, then my father.

"We are going to have the absolute best time," Aliyah says in the loudest voice possible as she takes hold of my hand and leads me up the stairs of her very own private jet. These people really do live a different life from the one I'm used to.

"We are." I smile while trying to mimic her level of enthusiasm.

I can tell by the look on her face that I don't succeed. The best thing about Aliyah, though, is the fact she doesn't pry. Instead, she steps into the jet and starts showing me around, pointing out everything and anything she can think of.

We get settled in the oversized luxury recliners and a stewardess brings us each a glass of champagne. "Here's to making great new memories to replace the shitty old ones," Aliyah says before tapping her glass against mine.

"Here's to new friends and new adventures." I smile, because this time, I really mean my words. "We are going to have the best time."

Liliana steps onto the plane, followed by a man. No, not just a man, a huge, six-foot-something man. I stiffen. I don't know why I get nervous around males I don't know. Okay, I do know why. Andrew fucked me up. His abuse wasn't just physical; it was also mental and long-lasting.

"Hey, sorry we're late. *This one* had to stare in the mirror for an hour before he'd leave the bathroom." Liliana points to the hulking shadow behind her.

"That, I believe. But damn, Enzo, if I wasn't

181

already married, I'd tell you that, that hour was well spent." Aliyah laughs. She's not wrong. I might not want to be anywhere near the guy, but even I can admit he's hot. I mean, not Luke kind of hot, but hot all the same.

"And if I had a death wish, I'd let you see more. You know, so you could truly appreciate the art of all *this*." The guy motions a hand up and down his suit-clad body. "But I don't, so eyes off the candy, Mrs. King."

"Gross. I'm sorry, Montana. This moron is my cousin, Enzo. He's tagging along with us. But don't worry, you'll barely notice he's here." Liliana plops down on the seat in front of Aliyah and me.

Enzo leans down and kisses Aliyah on the cheek. My body tenses at his sudden proximity. Aliyah takes hold of my hand and squeezes it. And then the guy sits next to Liliana.

"Hi, it's nice to meet you," he says while making no attempt to reach out and touch me. No handshake or anything, which I'm grateful for. His eyes are assessing me, though. I can tell he knows something isn't right.

"You too," I reply, keeping my voice light.

"She's a nervous flier," Aliyah chimes in. I'm not, but I appreciate the little white lie.

"I don't love it either, but I pulled the short straw and got stuck following Lil and her boyfriend around the world this week." Enzo shrugs.

"I didn't make the stupid rule of traveling in pairs," Liliana says. "You should talk to the oldies about that."

"And deny you the pleasure of my company? Never." He laughs, and the more I watch the two interact, the more my body relaxes. "So, Jameson, huh? You do know you're way too good for him?"

I realize the question is directed at me. "I am?" I'm not, but this guy doesn't know me.

"Fuck yeah, you are. If he doesn't treat you right, call me. I know people who know people." Enzo winks.

Liliana shoves an elbow into his arm. "Shut up. Don't scare her," she hisses under her breath.

"No, I'm interested. What kind of people are we talking about? The ones who can, you know, make someone disappear?" I lift my eyebrows up and down.

"If that's what you want." Enzo nods. "It'd be harder with a public figure like Jameson, but not impossible," he adds.

"What if it wasn't him? Like, let's say, *hypothetically*, I wanted to get rid of someone else?" Truth is I would love nothing more than to be rid of Andrew. I have no idea where he is or when he's going to pop up. I just know that he will.

"I could make it happen."

"How much does something like that cost a person?" I press.

"Okay, first of all, you're my friend. If you want someone offed, I'd get my brother to do it and you wouldn't pay a single dime. And second, she's joking, Enzo. So stop encouraging her," Aliyah says.

"I'd do it for free too. Just saying. Give me a name and I'll make it look like the fucker never existed," Enzo tells me, and I force a small smile.

"She's right. I was joking." *Mostly.*

As much as I'd love to give him Andrew's name, I'm not sure I could actually live with that on my conscience for the rest of my life. He doesn't deserve anything less than a cruel death, but it won't be at my hands, or at my instruction. It'll be karma that gets him in the end. I have to believe that.

"Offer's always there," Enzo says before plugging in a pair of earbuds as if he didn't just agree to murder someone for me.

The rest of the flight is spent drinking champagne. By the time the jet lands and we're walking down the steps, I'm more than just a little tipsy. It's been a long time since I've had this. *Friends.* I do, however, manage to make it off the plane in one piece without tripping.

I smile proudly at myself when my feet hit the tarmac. "I did it."

"You did." Aliyah wraps an arm around mine. "Now, can we make it to that car?" She points at the big black SUV ahead of us while Liliana grabs on to my other side.

"I think we can," she says, her words slurring slightly.

"You three are going to put me in an early grave. We've only just touched down and you're all wasted already." Enzo waves a hand in our direction.

"Not wasted. Just... a little more than tipsy," I correct him.

"What she said. Stop pouting, Enzo. It's not hot." Aliyah laughs as we all stumble towards the car before practically falling inside.

"It's so bright, so pretty. Who knew Vegas had so many lights?" I say while staring out the window.

"Everyone." Liliana laughs.

"Probably," I say, then press a finger to the glass. "Aw, look! There's one of those Elvis wedding chapels. You could get married."

"No, she fucking can't. Not on my watch. Don't

do any such thing, Liliana. Your father will kill me," Enzo growls.

"No, he won't." Liliana rolls her eyes. "Besides, your parents got married here."

"*You* are not my parents. And Zio Theo is not as forgiving as Nonno."

"Don't worry, I'm not doing the whole Vegas wedding thing. But it would be fun," Liliana tells me.

"It would," I agree.

We pull up to the front of a hotel and the car door is opened. I have no idea where we are. All I know is that Luke said the team booked out a few floors and had a lot of security hanging around. Aliyah, who seems to have sobered up more than the rest of us, checks everyone in. She holds up two keys, handing one to me and then one to Liliana.

"I've had a dress put in each of your rooms. You have an hour to get changed, glam up, and meet me at that bar over there." She gestures behind us.

"An hour?" Liliana parrots.

"*An hour.* Don't be late. I've planned a night of fun. We're in Vegas, bitches. It's time to party!" Aliyah screams.

"Okay. Let's do this." I nod. "I can do this," I say quietly to myself as we all pile into the elevator.

Chapter Twenty-Two

I've been stuck in practice and meetings all day. I know Montana is here. We've been messaging back and forth. When she got to the room, she sent me a picture of her in a dress—well, I'm guessing it was a dress. She asked if she could wear it, saying Aliyah bought it for her and she didn't know if it was okay.

My reply was simple. I told her she didn't need my permission to wear something. And I told her if she liked it, then she should wear it. I followed that up with making sure she knew just how fucking amazing she looked in the little black glittery dress.

I understand I have to be patient. That it's going to take time for her to regain control of her life again. But every time she asks if she can do something, it reminds me of the hell she's lived in for the past three years.

"Has Vinny found anything yet?" I ask Gray as we walk out of the arena, towards his car.

"Nothing. It's like the guy's a ghost," he says.

"Let's hope he is," King grunts from behind us.

"And take away my fun?" I glance at him over one shoulder. "No, I want to make sure that fucker feels every bit of pain he inflicted on her—and more. I want him begging for his life."

"We all do," Gray says.

These guys have my back. I have no doubt about that. But no one wants to see that fucking weasel Andrew screaming in pain more than I do. Well, except maybe Montana.

I wonder if she'd do it. If she thought she could end him, would she?

I haven't mentioned that I have people looking for him. I want to be able to tell her that I found him first. That he's no longer a threat to her because he's no longer breathing. I want her to be able to sleep at night without waking up screaming. I want her to know peace again. To be happy and content, and not doubt her decisions every other second of the day. But I also know that will all take time. And I won't be the one rushing her.

We pull up to the front of the hotel, and I jump out and head straight for the bar.

"I'm gonna stop by my room and call Kathryn and Graycee. I'll catch up with you guys in a bit," Gray says.

I give him a nod and King and I keep walking. It takes less than a second to spot her inside the bar. It's not like it's hard. Montana fucking stands out like a siren. She's stunning.

I make a beeline for her, wrap my arm around her waist from behind, lean down, and whisper into her ear. "I fucking missed you."

The moment she hears my voice, her body relaxes into mine. Montana turns in her seat. Her arms circle my neck and her lips press against my mouth. "Probably not as much as I missed you."

"More," I say, briefly kissing her again. "You look fucking stunning. Breathtaking. Beautiful." I step back, holding her arm out and twirling her around so I get the full view.

"Thanks." She gives me a shy smile.

"You know you're crashing girls' night, right?" Liliana huffs.

"I don't care," I tell her.

She glances behind me and then around the bar. "Where's Travis?"

I look to King. Travis said he wanted to stop by a store to pick something up for his girl. We have no idea what, but he did ask us not to spoil the surprise. So I shrug a shoulder and try to play it off. "Last I checked, I wasn't his keeper. You were."

"Guy's getting up there in age, Lil. Takes him a little longer to change, shower, and dress himself after practice, you know," King adds.

"You two are hiding something." Liliana directs an accusatory finger from me to King. "You're both shit at lying. What's he doing?"

"No clue." I shrug again.

"Enzo, do your thing. Torture the information out of them," Liliana tells her cousin.

"Pass," he says. "Pick up your phone and call him like a normal person, Lil."

"Now there's a rational solution to your problem." King's laughter is cut off when Aliyah slaps his chest.

Then she turns to Liliana. "Okay, go find Travis. Tell him to get his ass here, or we're leaving without him."

"Where are we going?" I ask.

"To see a show." She smiles.

When Aliyah said we were going to see a show, I don't know what I thought it would be, but burlesque wasn't it. Montana is smiling, though. She's enjoying herself and that's all I care about.

"I love your smile," I tell her.

"Thank you." She leans into my side.

"I want to see it. Every day. Forever." I kiss her temple and she looks up at me.

"Forever is a long time, Luke," she whispers.

"When it comes to you, forever is not nearly long enough," I say, before an idea comes to mind and I grab her hand. "Let's go."

Without a thought, Montana follows me out of our seats. "Where to?" she asks as I lead her through the theater.

"I want to do something."

"Okay."

The moment we step onto the street, I turn left with a certain destination in mind. "You know I love you, right?" I ask her as we navigate the crowded Vegas sidewalk.

"I know. I love you too."

"And you know that you are it for me. You always have been and always will be."

"Okay..."

I stop walking as soon as we're standing in front of the little chapel I spotted on the way to the hotel. And look into Montana's eyes. "I want to do this, but only if you really want to do it too. You can say no. I'll still be here. I'll wait until you're ready, and if you're never ready, I'll still wait."

"Do what? Luke? What's going on?" I see the concern knitting her brows. She still doesn't understand what I'm asking her.

"Marry me," I clarify, then quickly add, "Please."

Montana gasps. "What? Have you been drinking?"

"No, I haven't had a drop of alcohol. I want to do this, Tanna. I've always wanted to do this," I tell her. "Marry me, right here, right now. Just the two of us."

"You're serious?"

"Never been more serious about anything. Marry me, Tanna," I ask again, and she grins.

"Yes."

I blink at her. "Yes?" I question, unsure if I heard her say it in my head or in real life.

"Yes," Montana repeats. "I've wanted to marry you forever, Luke. But I... What if I don't get better?"

"You are perfect, Montana. There is not a single thing wrong with you. I will love you forever. I promise. I will always be here to help chase away any demons that haunt you."

"I don't deserve you," she says as her eyes drop to her feet.

I reach out and tip her chin up until her gaze meets mine again before gesturing to the building behind us. "We deserve each other. Now, are you ready to become Mrs. Jameson?"

I'll call in a favor with Gray and ask him to get the paperwork in order when we get back to Vancouver. He has people who will make sure this marriage is legit.

"I was born ready." Montana smiles, and I lean

in and kiss her like no one is watching. Because, right now, it's just me and her. Us. Everything else blurs into the background.

"We're really doing this," Montana says, her hands locked in mine as we stand on an altar in front of an Elvis impersonator.

"We are, but we can do the big fancy wedding too," I remind her.

"I don't need that. I just need you."

"Okay, you folks ready?" Elvis asks.

"Yes," Montana and I say at the same time.

"Great. Luke, are you ready to take Montana here as your wife?" Elvis asks me.

"I am," I tell him before he turns to Montana.

"Montana, are you ready to take Luke here as your husband?"

"I am," she says.

"Okay, Luke, you wanted to say your own vows. The stage is yours." Elvis nods in my direction and takes a step back.

"Montana, I have loved you for my entire life. I

have been *in* love with you for almost just as long. I don't want one lifetime with you. I want a million lifetimes with you. I promise to always put you above anything else. I promise to cherish you. To not only be your husband but also your best friend. Forever. I promise to give you a life filled with happiness, love, friendship. But most of all, safety. I will always be your biggest fan. Whatever you want to do, whatever you want to achieve, I'll be right behind you supporting you how ever I can. I don't need to promise to love you forever, because that's a given."

"Montana, is there anything you'd like to say to Luke?" Elvis asks.

"Yes." Montana takes a deep breath, closes her eyes, then opens them again. "Luke, I don't know what I would do without you. You are my everything. You give me strength when I don't have any. You love me even when I don't feel worthy of that love. You are my best friend. You are the love of my life, and that's something no one can ever take away. Each moment I spend with you, I can feel myself coming back to life. I can't wait to spend every day in this lifetime and the next with you. I love you. I don't know the right words to express that, but know that I do."

Everything else happens fast. Rings are slid onto

fingers. And more words are exchanged until the one sentence I've waited so long to hear resonates louder than all the rest.

"I now pronounce you... man and wife. You may kiss your bride."

My arms immediately wrap around Montana as I pick her up and slam my lips onto hers before spinning her around. "Mrs. Jameson, I fucking love you," I tell her as I set her feet on the ground.

"I love you too." She smiles up at me.

We walk out of the chapel and the flashes of light momentarily blind me. Multiple flashes. Over and over again. Montana shrinks behind me and I circle an arm around her shoulder. I do my best to block her, hide her face from all the cameras.

Where the fuck did they even come from?

Ignoring the flurry of questions being tossed my way, I walk down the street and into the first open hotel I see. It's not the one we're staying at, but it'll do. The paps can't follow us in here.

Chapter Twenty-Three

Oh my god. What on earth is happening? There are cameras, so many cameras. My face is going to be plastered all over the tabloids. I was just photographed walking arm in arm out of a wedding chapel with Luke Jameson. The NHL's number one bachelor.

Shit. What do I do? I don't know what to do. I need to fix this. He's going to see it. He's going to find me.

"Tanna, calm down. It's going to be okay. Count with me: one, two, three, four, five..." Luke says, and I try to focus on his words instead of the mess inside my head. When he gets to the number six, he starts back at one again.

"I'm sorry. I'm so sorry," I tell him.

"It's okay. I don't know how they knew we were there." He sighs while raking a hand over his face. "But it's going to be okay."

"No, it's not." I can feel the tears running down my cheeks but there's nothing I can do to stop them. "He's going to see it, the pictures. He's going to know. He's going to find me." I heave in a breath. My chest is heavy, weighed down by that feeling of being held under water. I'm struggling to breathe.

"I won't let anyone hurt you, Tanna. I promise." Luke kisses the top of my forehead.

"I'm not worried about what he'll do to me, Luke. He's going to go after you. He warned me what would happen if I talked to you. And I didn't just talk to you. I married you."

"I know. And there are no take backs, Tanna. You're my wife. And you know what? The world needs to know that. We'll increase security, but don't worry about me, babe. I'm a big boy."

"I can't lose you, Luke. I can't."

"You won't ever lose me. I'm yours, always," he says while wrapping his arms around me again.

The weight on my chest starts to seep away. Slowly. Very slowly. I cling to him like my life depends on it, though. I don't want to let him go. And Luke? He just stands here, holding me, ensuring I'm the first to break away. He never rushes me. He's so damn patient, so damn perfect. And so mine. I won't let anyone take this from me now. I've just got him back and I'm not giving him up without a fight.

"What do we do now?" I ask, looking towards the door. I can't go back out there into that shitstorm.

"We're going to get a room and consummate this marriage. All of this..." He gestures to the door and the chaos just outside. "... can wait until tomorrow."

With my hand clasped firmly in his, Luke leads me up to the reception desk. He requests their best room and hands over his credit card. I don't listen to whatever else is said. I'm too busy taking in the environment and recalling the vows we just exchanged.

Well, that and trying to tamp down the building anticipation for what the rest of the night entails. My thighs press together. It's probably a bit messed up that I can go from having a mild panic attack to being a wanton, horny mess in a matter of minutes.

Maybe I should bring this up with Dr. West. I wonder what she'll say about my sudden nuptials?

But I'm not worried about what people will think about our spur-of-the-moment decision. I know I love Luke and I know he loves me too. I just never want to put him in a position where he'll have to choose between me and someone else he loves.

Shit, his parents.

"Luke, we have to call your parents," I say as soon as we enter the elevator.

"Why?"

"We just got married. Your mom is going to be pissed. Oh my god, she's going to hate me!" I gasp.

"No, she's not, and we will tell them. In person. We'll make a stop before we head home."

"What if they don't approve? I have a lot of baggage. Baggage your mother saw firsthand."

"I don't need anyone's approval, Tanna. You are my wife. Nothing is changing that."

I pray that he's right. I pray that he doesn't have to defend his choice to tie his life to mine.

"We should probably talk about visiting your father," Luke says after a moment of silence.

"Or we could not and get onto the consummating part?" I suggest.

"That sounds like a great idea." Luke scoops me up bridal-style when the elevator opens, before he walks down the hallway and taps a card to a door. Then he carries me into an extremely luxurious hotel room. Where he places me on the bed, his body covering mine. "I love you, Mrs. Jameson."

"I love you, Mr. Jameson."

"You and me. Always," he says as his lips brush against my mouth.

"Always," I repeat.

"Stand up. Let's get you out of this dress." Luke pushes to his feet before holding his hand out to me. I look down at myself.

"I can't believe I got married in black." I laugh.

"Wanna do it again? Get a white dress? Because I gotta be honest, babe. I'll marry you over and over. As many times as you'd like. Best fucking day of my life," Luke says with a grin.

"No need for a redo." I reach behind my back and unzip the dress. When the fabric falls to the floor, I'm left in nothing but a black lace thong and a pair of heels.

Luke inhales a sharp breath, his eyes glazing over. Filled with lust, heat, and love. So much love.

For me. That's when it hits me. I thought Andrew loved me because he never left. I honestly thought *that* was love. It wasn't. It never was.

This. The way Luke looks at me. Loves me. This is the kind of love I hope every woman gets to experience in their lifetime. It's the kind of love that lights up your world, even on the darkest of days. And I've had a lot of dark days.

I'm not dismissing the work I've put in during my sessions with Dr. West, but I know if it weren't for Luke, I would not be where I am today.

"I'm the luckiest guy alive," Luke says, taking a step back before gesturing to my underwear. "Take those off."

I pull my panties down my legs and am left standing in just my heels.

He points to my feet. "And those."

I step out of my shoes and kick them to the side.

"This," Luke says. "I've never seen you wearing anything more perfect."

"I'm not wearing anything." I lift my arms to cover my torso. Or at least attempt to.

"Wrong. You're wearing my ring." Luke steps forward, takes my hands, and pulls them down to my sides. "Never hide yourself from me. There isn't an inch of you that I don't love."

"Okay." I nod. I can't promise that I won't try to cover my body. There are parts of me I don't like being seen. Old scars I don't want to explain.

"I want you so badly." Luke trails his fingertips down my chest, over my stomach, until he reaches my pussy. Then he circles my clit. "I've never wanted anything more."

"What about hockey? You always wanted to play hockey."

"Nowhere near as much as how I want you right now. I need to be inside you, Tanna." His fingers travel farther down before he pushes one digit up into my opening. "You're so fucking wet." His mouth lands on my shoulder before moving along my neck. "Is this for me?" he whispers into my ear.

"Yes."

"Good. Because I want it all."

My hands tug at his shirt. I'm completely naked and he's still fully dressed. Something I plan on rectifying right now. "I want it off."

Luke removes his finger from inside me. I whimper at the sudden loss. But it's not for long. As soon as his shirt is flinging across the room, Luke's hands are on me again, his fingers inside me. My hands fumble on his belt. I'd be able to concentrate better if he weren't making my entire body light up with pleasure right now.

Did he go to a class on how to finger a vagina?

Getting his belt undone, I flick open the button on his slacks and then slide the zipper lower. My hand reaches into his boxers and closes around his length. It's so hard. The tip leaking precum. I glide my hand back and forth a few times, as Luke bites down on my neck.

"Fuck," he grunts. "I need to be inside you."

Taking a step forward, Luke gently lays me on the bed again, and then he shoves off his shoes and pants before settling between my thighs. The tip of his cock lines up with my entrance.

"Are you on birth control?" he asks.

I shake my head. "I was, but I didn't... I haven't taken the pills since..." I let my sentence trail off.

"I don't want to pull out, Montana. If you have an issue with that, you need to tell me. I will, if you want me to. But I really want to come inside my wife."

"I don't want you to pull out," I tell him. I want everything he has to give me.

Luke enters me, almost reverently. His eyes stay focused on mine. When he bottoms out, his body shudders. "I love you, so damn much."

"I love you too, but I'm not fragile, Luke. I'm not going to break. I want you to fuck me."

"I want to take my time," he says.

"And you can, next round. Right now, I want you to fuck me. Don't treat me like I'm going to break. Because I won't. Promise."

Without another word, Luke pulls out and slams back inside my pussy. And he fucks me. He doesn't stop when the first orgasm racks through my body. He keeps going. Until a second orgasm erupts and his own control snaps as he comes inside me.

Chapter Twenty-Four

I wake up to an incessant buzzing. Picking up my phone, I rub at my eyes, glance at the time, and shut off my alarm. Then I turn on my side and wrap an arm around Montana's naked body. My wife's naked body.

"Morning, wife." I kiss the back of her shoulder.

"This isn't morning, Luke. It's still dark out," she groans.

"I have to be at the arena in an hour," I tell her.

"Okay, but I don't."

"I want you to come with me," I say. "I'm not ready to let you go."

Montana rolls over to look at me. "Okay. But won't I just be in the way?"

"You could never be in the way." I lean in, planning to kiss her, until the noise of my phone ringing stops me. I let out an annoyed grunt as I eye the screen and slide the green answer button across when I see Aliyah's name. "Hey, Lia. I'm a little busy right now—"

"Luke Jameson, what have you done? Have you seen the news? Oh my god! My dad is having a fit right now. It's everywhere!" Aliyah practically screams down the line.

"What's everywhere?"

"You eloped with Montana last night. What were you thinking?"

"I was thinking that I love her and wanted to marry her," I say confidently.

"It's a scandal. The speculations are insane. Turn on the news. Actually, no, don't let her see it.

Shit. She's going to freak, Luke. This isn't good. Where are you?"

"Lia, calm down. It'll all be fine. This will blow over." The tabloid stories always do.

"This is huge. *Vancouver's number one bachelor officially off the market* kind of huge." Aliyah sighs. "Where are you? I'll come to you."

"We're at Planet Hollywood."

"Planet Hollywood? You're kidding me, right? Please, for the love of God, tell me you're joking?"

"No, why?"

"You took her to Planet Hollywood? Are times that tough, Jameson? You could have least taken her across the road to the Bellagio. I mean, seriously?" She continues to drone on.

"Okay, Aliyah, I'm hanging up," I tell her.

"Wait! What room number?"

It's on the tip of my tongue to tell her not to come here, but she's Montana's friend. And I have a feeling she might be able to help ease the panic that will set in when my new bride sees what's going on. I don't need to turn on the news outlets to know some of what they're saying.

Vancouver Knights cover up secret love child...

Number six blackmailed into shotgun wedding...

First a mysterious injury, now a mysterious bride. Sources say it's likely drug-related...

"Room 912," I huff into the phone.

"It's not even a penthouse suite. Oh my god."

I can hear the disapproval in Aliyah's tone. It doesn't matter, though, because I know Montana, and she couldn't care less about where we are as long as we're together. I cut the call and see my new wife waiting patiently for an update. "Aliyah is on her way over. We need to get dressed."

"What's happened?"

I look away. I don't want to tell her, but I don't want to lie to her either. "I don't want you to worry, Tanna. Whatever they're saying doesn't matter. All that matters is that you and I know the truth, our truth. We love each other."

"What who are saying?"

"The news outlets caught wind of our nuptials. It's all over the tabloids," I explain.

"Shit." She jumps up out of bed and runs into the bathroom. By the time I have my boxers and slacks on, Montana walks back out with a robe wrapped around her. "Okay, what do I do? Tell me what to do," she says.

"Are you okay?"

"No, but we're going to deal with this together, right?"

"Always together. You and me, Tanna."

"Okay, then tell me what I need to do."

"Don't say anything. If anyone approaches you, don't answer their questions. Don't let them bait you into getting angry or upset, because they will try. The paparazzi are nothing but a bunch of vultures. But I'm going to make sure you're never alone. I'm going to call Gray. Get him to send us a security detail."

"Okay. What if..." She doesn't finish her sentence.

"What if *what*?"

"What if he comes for me?" she asks. "I mean, I know him. He's going to see this and he's going to do something."

"I won't let him get anywhere near you, Tanna. I promise," I tell her.

"Okay, so just don't say anything. That's it? What should I wear? How should I do my hair?" She looks around the room, clearly distressed.

"Tanna, I don't care what you wear or how you do your hair. You don't need to dress to impress anyone but yourself."

"But if they're taking pictures... Luke, I don't want to embarrass you."

"You could never embarrass me." I wrap an arm around her waist and pull her tight against my body. "I love you. Never forget that."

"I love you too."

"I'm sorry you have to deal with this." I sigh before pressing a kiss to the top of her head.

"It's not half as bad as the baggage I'm bringing into this marriage. Everyone wants a piece of you, Luke. I can't fault them for that. Look at you." Montana peers up at me.

"You really are perfect."

"Thank you," she says at the same time there's a knock on the door and then it's opening.

"How'd you get a key?" I ask Aliyah, who's now walking into the room, followed by King, O'Neil, Gray, Liliana, and Enzo.

"Put on a shirt. No one needs to see all of that." Aliyah waves a hand at me. "I brought you some clothes. Thought you wouldn't want to walk out in last night's dress." Aliyah passes a bag to Montana before pulling her into a hug. "And we're doing this wedding thing again, properly. I want to be there. Also, congratulations. I'm so freaking happy for you.

You deserve this." She keeps her voice low, but not so low I can't hear her.

"Thank you," Montana says.

The guys all congratulate us before Gray's expression turns serious. "We have a game plan. I have more guys flying in. But until then, Montana's coming everywhere with us." I nod my agreement, and he adds, "Enzo will sit with her and the girls while we're in meetings or out on the ice."

I turn my attention to Enzo. "Thank you."

"No need to thank me," he says.

"Okay. You, shirt." Aliyah looks at me, then ushers Montana towards the bathroom. "You, go get changed."

I grab my shirt from the floor and slide my arms through the sleeves. When Montana walks out of the bathroom again, my heart stutters. She's wearing my jersey and a pair of jeans. Her hair is tied up in a high ponytail and her face is free of makeup. She takes my breath away.

"All right, when we walk out, stick between Luke and Gray," Aliyah says. "Oh, and here." She pulls a pair of sunglasses out of her bag before passing them to Montana. "The trick is to pretend they're not there. Think of them like annoying little ghosts who don't actually exist."

Montana takes a deep breath. "Okay. I guess we can't hide out in here forever, right?" She looks to me.

"I wouldn't mind." I raise my eyebrows at her.

"I bet you wouldn't. Now, come on. It's going to be fine. I've got this. Trust me, I managed to get the press to love Liam even after he was unlovable," Aliyah tells Montana.

"You loved me from the very first moment we met," King chimes in.

"It was like a real-life episode of *Naked and Afraid*." Aliyah laughs.

"Yeah, that's enough of that," Gray grunts as we all exit the hotel room.

Montana's hand is gripped firmly in mine. Liliana stops us the moment we hit the lobby. "Travis and I are going to go out first. We're going to make a scene and try to get them to follow us in the opposite direction," she says.

"You guys don't need to do that," I tell them.

"It's fine. I'm used to it. Besides, it'll be fun." Liliana smirks.

"I have to go with her. I'll meet you guys at the arena," Enzo says before following his cousin out the door. The moment they step foot outside, the flashes start up again.

Did those fuckers camp out all damn night? Probably. Like I said, they're nothing but fucking vultures waiting for a fresh carcass to pick at. And I refuse to let them have a taste of Montana.

Chapter Twenty-Five

I 'm sitting next to Aliyah and Liliana. Watching the team practice. I'm impressed by their stamina. Honestly, I'd be passed out on the floor by now. I'm exhausted just watching them run drills.

"Do you skate?" I ask Liliana. Aliyah already

told me she doesn't like going out on the ice. She has a fear of blades, but that's her story to tell, not mine.

"I can. I don't very often, though. Do you?"

"I used to. When we were kids, I'd follow Luke and Sean to the rink whenever I could. I mostly just wanted to hang out with them. But I got decent at skating at the same time."

"We should go to Gray and Kathryn's and skate with Graycee one day. She'd love it," Liliana says.

"Gray and Kathryn have a rink in their house?" I ask, shocked.

"Yeah, Gray put it in for Graycee. The guys run drills with her there all the time."

I've met Graycee. She's adorable *and* obsessed with all things hockey, particularly the Vancouver Knights. "That's insane but cute."

Money aside, I don't think my parents ever would have gone to that sort of effort for me.

I watch Luke and wonder what kind of father he'd be. Not that I want it to happen anytime soon. But eventually. When I'm better. When I can sleep without waking up screaming. Although, now that I think about it, I didn't have a nightmare last night.

I smile and grip Aliyah's arm. "I didn't wake up last night," I tell her excitedly. "I didn't have a nightmare."

"What do you have nightmares about?" Liliana chimes in.

I blink as I look at her. I haven't told her about my past, about how Luke only came to get me because his mother called him from the hospital after I'd been beaten up by my boyfriend.

"I, ah, I had an ex who wasn't the nicest person," I admit.

"That's who you wanted to put a hit out on? When you asked Enzo about it on the jet?" Liliana asks. "Give me a name and I'll call my dad right now and get it done."

I shake my head. "I can't. I know that he deserves it. And I want him to disappear, but I can't be the reason he does."

"Okay. Well, if you change your mind, you have my number." Liliana looks out towards the ice. "Do you think they get hard doing that? Like, do they imagine moving on top of someone while gyrating on the ice?"

I follow her line of sight and see the guys stretching. And she's right. Their routine is very... provocative.

"Think anyone would notice if I just got up and slid underneath Travis right now?" Liliana grins.

"Yeah, me." Enzo's voice comes from behind us, making me jump ten feet in the air.

My hand lands on my chest. "Shit, I forgot you were there."

"Sorry. Didn't mean to scare you." He pauses, attempting to appear casual when he asks, "Out of curiosity, what did you say the name of your ex was?"

"I didn't."

Enzo smiles at me. "You're smart. Told you that you were too good for Jameson."

"Agree to disagree." I smile at him. The more I'm around Liliana's cousin, the more comfortable I feel.

"Agree to disagree." Enzo laughs. "I like that."

I return my attention to the ice. Luke is staring at me. Or is he staring behind me?

I glance over my shoulder but Enzo's focus is on his phone. When I turn back to look at Luke, he waves me over to the edge of the rink. So I push to my feet and approach the barrier.

Did I do something wrong?

I shouldn't have been talking to Enzo. I keep letting myself fall into this false sense of normalcy. And I keep forgetting the rules. "I'm sorry. I didn't mean to. It won't happen again," I rush to say as soon as Luke is within earshot.

His brows draw down. "What are you sorry for?"

"For talking to another man. I shouldn't have done it. I know that. I shouldn't have..." I don't know what to say to get him to forgive me.

"Tanna, I don't care who you talk to. If you want to talk to Enzo, then talk to him. He's a good guy."

"You don't care?" I ask, the concept a little farfetched if I'm being honest.

"No, I don't," Luke says while pulling his helmet off his head.

"Then why did you look mad?"

"Because you're cold. I can tell you're cold and I should have gotten you a jacket." He sighs. "I'm not mad at you, Tanna. I'm pissed at myself for not considering your needs before bringing you here. I have to do better."

"I'm fine. I'm not that cold," I tell him. Or more like swoon at his feet. Could this man be any more perfect? I think not.

"Lia?" he calls out.

"Luke, don't. It's fine. I'm not that cold. I swear!" I tell him.

"What's up?" Aliyah calls back from her seat.

"Can you ask someone to bring Montana a coat?"

"You don't have to do that," I insist. "It's fine."

"You're cold and you don't need to be. You

shouldn't have to be. Let me do this for you. Please," Luke says.

"I already did. About five minutes ago. I got all of us one, Montana. Don't worry." Aliyah smiles at me.

"Oh, thank you."

"I'm sorry I didn't think about it sooner," Luke says.

"Luke, you're not my father. I don't need you to look after my every need," I tell him.

"I'm your husband, and that's what husbands do. They tend to their wives every need." His voice has dropped a pitch. It's more husky. Growly.

My thighs clench together and my clit throbs at his hidden message. "You need to get back out there." I nod behind him.

"Yeah, I do." He sighs. "Are you sure you're okay? You don't need anything?" His eyes travel the length of my body before returning to my face.

"What I need you can't give me right now. So, yes, I'm okay."

"What is it that you need, Tanna?" he asks.

I lean forward and press my lips to his ear. "I need my husband to fuck me," I tell him. "I need one of those orgasms only he can give me." I step back and watch my words wash over him.

"Fuck my job. Giving you what you need is far more important," he grunts.

"Don't you dare. Nope, I came to Vegas to watch you play, Luke Jameson. Don't even think about walking off that ice. Besides, you can make sure I get what I want tonight, *after* you win."

"I'd much rather give it to you now," he pouts.

"I know. But we can wait. We have the rest of our lives together, Luke. We can wait a few hours."

"And the next," he reminds me before skating off.

"And the next," I repeat to myself.

I sit back down between Aliyah and Liliana, and a few minutes later, a girl walks out with three Vancouver letterman jackets.

Aliyah passes one to each of us. "We're going to need these. It's freaking cold in this place."

"Thank you," I tell her.

We're in a private box now. I don't know how Aliyah got us a last-minute box, but she did. And I'm grateful I don't have to be down *there* with the crowd. The game is in the third period. We're up by one, and I'm on the edge of my seat, waiting for the timer to go off. There are still five minutes on the clock. And, honestly, anything could happen.

"Please let them win," I pray to something, to anyone listening.

"They're going to win." Aliyah nods.

"From your lips to God's ears," Liliana adds.

Three minutes on the clock. The Vegas team gets the puck and I see it before it happens. They slap it past our goalie and tie the score.

"Looks like we're going into overtime," Aliyah comments. "No one is going to beat the dream trio in overtime."

"The dream trio?" I ask her.

"Liam, Gray, and Luke." She grins. "Their line is practically undefeated in overtime."

"Practically?"

"They've lost once or twice, but we don't talk about those instances. There's no room for negativity in this life. So, bring on the overtime. We're going to win."

I wish I had her confidence. It's not that I don't think the Knights are a great team. They are. But so is Vegas. And, well, I'm nervous. Luke takes the losses hard. He'll spend hours watching the replays, trying to see where things went wrong. What he could have done better.

No one else knows he does that. Well, no one but Grayson, because he does it too.

I get that losing is part of the game. Part of the sport. But Luke is my husband, and I'm allowed to want him to only experience winning, right? I haven't been a wife for all that long, but surely that's on the list of things a wife can do?

I wonder if there is an actual list. I should ask Aliyah.

The second I think it, I also realize how stupid I'm being. There's no list. As Luke likes to remind me, I am the decision-maker in my own life. There are no rules, other than the ones I set for myself. I get to decide what I do and when I do it. I get to decide the kind of life I want to live and no one has the power to make me think or do otherwise.

Chapter Twenty-Six

The game's gone into overtime. We're at the shootout stage. O'Neil is up first. We're all waiting, ready to jump the boards if he scores.

I watch as he skates towards the net. He fakes a left, then a right. And as the goalie leans to one side,

O'Neil contorts his body in an inhuman way to slap the puck to the left again. That little black disc flies right over the goalie's right glove and hits the back of the net.

"Fuck yeah!" I yell. Jumping over the boards, rushing towards Travis, and landing on his back. "Yes!" I slap his shoulder while the rest of the team piles on top of us. "You did it."

Anyone would think we just won the Cup, but the thing about the Knights is we treat every game like it's the playoffs. And this year, we *will* be returning. We will be keeping that title in Vancouver.

After all the presentations, I finally get to hit the showers. I can't wait to get back to my wife. I want to take her to the hotel and spend the night celebrating this win with her, preferably buried between her legs.

Montana is waiting with Liliana and Enzo when I walk out of the locker room. "Everything okay?" I ask, my eyes flicking between the three of them.

"Everything's good. Where you heading now?" Enzo says.

"The hotel." I look from Enzo to Montana. "Unless you wanted to go somewhere else?"

She bites her bottom lip. "No, I'm really tired. The hotel is exactly where I want to go."

I take Montana's hand in mine and smile before turning to Liliana. "Where are you guys headed?"

"I'm waiting for Travis. He's following you two back to the hotel," she says.

"You sure? You don't have to do that," I reply as Gray walks out of the locker room to join us.

"Yeah, I'll come. There's a circus of paps out front," Enzo tells me.

"Okay. Appreciate it."

"We're going in through the back," Gray says. "I've already made the arrangements. A driver's picking us up now."

I don't know what I'd do without my friends. I mean, I'd hire security for Montana, of course. There's no amount of money I wouldn't spend to keep her safe. That much I know. But their support is invaluable. It's nice knowing these guys have our backs.

Once we're in the car, Montana turns to Gray. "I have a favor to ask."

"You do?" he replies, looking just as shocked as I feel.

"I heard you have an ice rink in your house, and I was kind of wondering if I could see it," Montana clarifies.

"That's not a favor," Gray tells her. "Luke has keys. He can bring you 'round whenever you want."

"You guys have keys to each other's homes?" Montana looks between us. "Is this the kind of bromance where I'm going to have to share my husband's time with you?" She directs the question to Gray.

"Absolutely, fucker couldn't last a day without me," he deadpans.

"Fuck off. I could live plenty fine without seeing your ugly mug," I tell him, then turn in my seat to look at Montana. "If you want an ice rink, I'll build you one of your own. But first... say it again."

"I don't want one." She laughs. "I was just curious. I've never seen an ice rink inside someone's house before. And say what again?"

"Who am I to you?"

"My husband." She smiles at me.

"That. That's what I wanted to hear. I love hearing you say that." I lean over, grip her chin between my thumb and index finger, and drop my mouth to hers. If we were alone in this car, I'd have her moaning beneath me in minutes. But we're not, and I don't like to share.

Montana is nervous, scared, and I can tell she'd rather be literally anywhere but back in our hometown. Gray arranged to have the Monroe jet make a detour so we could stop here before returning to Vancouver.

We've just left my parents' place. I haven't brought up visiting her father again. I think that's something we can discuss another day. When she's ready. There is one other stop I need to make though. And I really don't know how Montana will feel about it. Although I get my answer as soon as the car pulls into the cemetery.

"Why are we here?" she asks.

"I need to talk to Sean." I watch her face, looking for the slightest hint of discomfort.

"Why? You do know he can't hear you, right?"

"Maybe, maybe not. But I just married his baby

sister, and I need to tell him. You want to come with me?" I hold out my hand when I step down from the car, more than a little surprised when Montana accepts the offer. Honestly, I thought she'd opt to stay behind.

"I've been writing to him," she admits as we make our way through the cemetery towards Sean's headstone. "In my journal."

"Do you think it helps?"

"I don't know."

"Well, it can't hurt, right?" I say, stopping when I spot his name in stone. A wave of emotions hits me. I haven't been back here since he was put in the ground. I didn't trust myself enough to risk seeing her again. "Did you come here a lot?" It's clear the site has been well cared for.

"At first, I did. I, um, after the third time Andrew hit me, I came here. I begged Sean for help. Like I said, he can't hear you." Montana won't look me in the eye.

My hand tightens around hers. "I'm sorry." I pull her closer to me and my arm wraps around her shoulder. "I don't even know where to start," I admit.

"Just say whatever's on your mind. Who knows? Maybe he'll listen to you?" She smiles. "He might have just been busy when I came. I bet they have the best ice up in heaven."

"I fucking hope so." I laugh.

Dropping my arm from her shoulders, I take hold of her hand again and together we kneel in front of his headstone. I try to find the words, try to figure out how to tell him what I need to say.

"I know you're not going to approve or like what I'm about to tell you, but you're going to have to find a way to get over it. Because this is real. I married Tanna, Sean. I guess that makes us brothers now. I would have loved for you to have been there. She looked beautiful. She *is* beautiful. But I needed you to hear it from me. I don't know if there's like angel gossip lines or whatever, but I didn't want to risk you finding out from someone else." I sigh, running my free hand through my hair. "I should have told you how much in love with your sister I was when you were here. Who knows? Maybe if I did, a lot of things would have turned out differently." I glance across to Montana. She gives me a reassuring smile so I keep going. "I want you to know that I'm going to look after her. I'm going to love her right, Sean. I promise I won't let anyone hurt her ever again."

"Sean, I love him and he makes me happy. He

treats me right. Don't be too hard on him," Montana says.

We sit here for a few minutes, silently holding hands. And when I feel the first drops of rain, I bring Montana up to her feet as I stand. "Thank you for doing this with me," I tell her.

"You and me together, always, right?"

"Always." I lean in and kiss her.

The sound of a gunshot has me pulling away from her mouth. Montana gasps for breath as I pick her up and run for the car, where Gray is holding the back door open for us. Just as I reach him, another shot sounds out, and I practically throw Montana to safety. As soon as the door is closed behind Gray, the SUV screeches out of the cemetery. It's only then that I look at Montana. Her face is pale, and she's holding a blood-covered hand over her stomach.

"No!" I scream and my vision blurs. No. This isn't happening. "We need a fucking hospital, now." I don't know who I'm telling, but I do hear Gray give the driver directions. My hand covers Montana's. "It's going to be okay. You're going to be okay, Tanna. You are going to be okay," I repeat.

"I love you," she says, her voice quiet.

"No, you stay awake, Tanna. Do not go to sleep. Don't leave me," I plead with her.

"I love you, Luke." She heaves a breath. "Always. Thank you for marrying me." Her voice is a whisper as her eyes close.

"No, Tanna! Please wake up." I scoop her onto my lap. "Drive faster. We need a fucking doctor!" I yell out while holding Montana's lifeless body against my chest.

Chapter Twenty-Seven

"What are you doing, Tanna?" The voice has me spinning around.

"Sean?" I question. I mean, it looks like my brother. But how did he get here? And where is here? I look around the room. It's all white. As far as I can see, it's just white.

"You're not supposed to be here yet, Tanna," he says, walking closer to me.

"It's really you?" I close the distance and throw my arms around his neck. "I've missed you so much."

"I've missed you too." He holds me tight to his chest for a moment longer. "But you shouldn't be here."

"Where is here?" I ask aloud this time, while taking a step back to look around again.

"Heaven. You need to go back before it's too late, Tanna."

I shake my head. "I'm not leaving you. I need you. There's so much you've missed."

"I haven't missed a thing," he says. "Luke needs you more than I do. He needs you to fight, Tanna. He needs you back."

All the anger I've felt towards my brother for what he did, how he left me, rises to the surface. "You left. Why the hell did you leave me? I needed you and you left. Why, Sean? Why would you do that to me? To us?" I yell as my hands slam against his chest.

"I didn't. I didn't slice my own wrists, Tanna. Not willingly. I would have never left you like that. It was..."

"She's back," another voice calls out as I'm taken

out of the white room and thrown somewhere else. There's a lot of noise. Machines. People everywhere.

What's happening?

"Let's get her into the OR now," I hear someone shout, and then I'm moving.

"Where are you taking her? She's my wife!" That's Luke.

I try to yell for him, and I look around but I don't see him.

No! I need to go back. I was with Sean. I need to go back. I need to know what he was going to say! What did he mean when he said he didn't do it?

My vision blurs, my eyelids get heavy to the point I can't keep them open any longer, and I let myself fall into the darkness.

"Sean, where are you?" I call out to the empty white room. I know he's here. He was here before. He has to be here now too.

"Tanna, fight, damn it," Sean says, appearing in front of me again.

"Like you did?" I throw back at him.

"I didn't have a choice. You do."

"What do you mean? What happened?" I ask him. "Tell me what happened?"

"Mom," he says, and I frown.

What would our mother have to do with this? We haven't seen or heard from her since we were kids. She left us. She chose another life.

"What do you mean *Mom*?"

"I found her."

"Where is she?" Why would he look for her? She didn't want us. Why should we want her?

"No. You don't need to know that." Sean shakes his head.

"Sean, tell me what's happening! Tell me what happened to you!" I scream at him.

"You have to go back. You're running out of time, Tanna," he says, instead of answering me.

"No, not until you tell me."

"I did it to protect you. It was supposed to protect you. I didn't know... I didn't know it wouldn't." Sean steps closer and takes my hand. "I'm sorry. I tried to protect you and I failed."

"What do you mean? How does you dying protect me? It doesn't, Sean. You broke my heart."

"You have Luke. He'll do a better job than I ever

could. Tell him to break out. He'll know what it means, what to do."

"You're not making any sense." I shake my head from side to side. None of this makes any sense.

"He'll understand it. Just tell him. When you wake up, tell him those words, Tanna."

"You should tell him yourself."

"Tanna, I'm sorry."

"No, this isn't real. You are not real. This is a dream or something." I turn around and look out into the depths of the never-ending whiteness.

"Go back, Tanna. You need to fight," Sean says from behind me. But when I turn back around, he's gone.

"What if I don't want to fight anymore?" I whisper to the void. It doesn't reply. So I sit down. There's nothing here. No noise, no view, just nothingness. It's kind of numbing. And, honestly, I like it. I could just stay here. I don't need to keep fighting. I'm tired.

How much should one person have to fight in a lifetime? I have no idea, but I've had enough of it. I just want peace. Why can't I find peace?

I close my eyes and a vision comes to mind. It's me and Luke. We're in his house, our house, sitting on the sofa in the theater room. He's watching crappy reality television with me while his hand is on my protruding stomach. "I think it's a girl," he says.

"Oh yeah? What makes you think that?" I ask him.

"Because earth needs more angels, and a mini-you is the purest fucking thing I can think of." He kisses my stomach. "You are an angel," he says to our unborn child.

"I think you hold me up on an extremely unrealistic pedestal. I'm not perfect, Luke."

"You are," he says. "When can we do this again?"

"Do what? Watch *The Real Housewives*?"

"No, this?" He rubs my stomach. "Have a baby."

I laugh. "How about we get through birthing the first one before you try to knock me up again?"

My body is shifted to another time. A new vision. At the rink. Luke is skating with a little girl, and I'm holding a baby. A boy.

Luke skates up to me. "Hey, Mama, pass him over."

"Do not drop him, Luke Jameson," I warn as I clutch the tiny bundle closer to my chest.

"You know I do this for a living, right?" He points to his skates.

"I also watch you hit the ground a lot while earning that living," I remind him.

"Mama, can we take Sean, pweease." The little girl looks up at me with eyes so like my husband's. "I'll help."

"Okay, but only for a little bit, Aubrey," I tell her before passing the infant over to Luke.

I watch, and a smile tugs at my face as the three of them skate off together.

My eyes spring open and all I can see is nothingness again. "I have to go back," I think aloud. I want that life with Luke, so I have to go back.

Chapter Twenty-Eight

I thought I had experienced pain in my life. I was wrong. Having my wife die in my arms is the worst kind of pain imaginable. A desperation unlike anything I've ever known had me praying, had me offering my own soul in place of hers.

When we finally got to the hospital, Montana's

body was taken from me. I didn't want to let her go but I also knew I needed to let the doctors save her. I couldn't do it alone.

She's been in surgery for hours now. How long does it take to remove a bullet?

A fucking bullet. My wife was shot. The back of my head hits the wall. I've been sitting in the same spot since I watched them wheel her off. On the floor, in the hallway where I last saw her. I've watched doctors and nurses come and go. But none of it seems to register. I can't feel anything but the gaping hole in my chest.

She has to be okay. She's strong. She's a survivor.

"She's going to pull through," Gray says from beside me. He hasn't left. He's been sitting here the entire time too.

"She has to," I tell him. "I can't lose her."

"You won't." His phone rings, and he looks down at the screen. "It's Vinny. I gotta take this." Gray eyes me warily before pushing to his feet and walking down the hall a bit.

He doesn't have to worry. I'm not going anywhere. Where would I go when the other half of my soul is somewhere through those doors?

My mom and dad have been here for the last two hours, coming to check on me every few minutes or so. Mom clears her throat. "You should come and sit in the waiting room, Luke."

"I'm not moving. Why is it taking so long?"

"It's normal for surgeries to take this long," Mom says, but I can tell she's holding something back. There's something she's not saying. I don't want to hear it, though. I can't hear that Montana's chances of pulling through are slim. I don't want to hear that she might not make it.

I carried her dead body in here, and then I watched them bring her back. They can save her. They already did.

"Son, don't give up hope. She's in good hands and she's a fighter. We all know that," my dad says.

"I know," I tell him.

"I'm going to get you a coffee," Mom says before walking back down the hall. My dad follows behind her.

I don't tell them that I won't drink it. I can't stomach anything right now. I stare down at my hands, Montana's blood still staining my skin. I should get up and rinse it off, but I can't move.

"Managed to get CCTV footage from the cemetery. Vinny's running through it now," Gray says as he drops down beside me again.

"I'm going to kill him. It has to be Andrew. Who else would do this to her?"

"My money would be on Andrew too, but we'll know for sure soon," Gray says. "And then we'll find the fucker."

"She died. She fucking died." My voice is hoarse, my eyes burning. I won't cry, though, because she's going to be okay.

"I know." Gray grips my shoulder with one of his hands and squeezes. "We will find whoever the fuck did this, Luke. I swear it."

"What's happening?" Aliyah's voice paired with the clicking of heels has us looking up at her.

"What are you doing here?" Gray asks.

"Shut up. Where is she, Luke? What are they doing?"

"She's still in surgery." What else can I say? That my entire world is hitched on the skills of whatever fucking surgeon is currently digging around for a piece of lead in my wife's body?

"She's okay, right?" Aliyah kneels down in front of me. "She's okay, Luke. She will be," she says more firmly.

"She will be," I repeat, even if my heart doesn't believe it one hundred percent. "She has to be."

"You need anything?" King asks from where he's standing behind Aliyah.

I shake my head. I appreciate that they're all here. But there's not much any of us can do but hope.

My mom walks up a few minutes later and hands me a coffee cup. I take it from her hands and place it next to me. "Thanks, Mom."

I don't look up again until another set of footsteps approaches our group. A surgeon, judging by the scrubs, with a grim look on his face. My stomach sinks. I've seen how this goes in the movies. The whole *we did everything we could* spiel. I can't hear that. I won't.

But instead of running past him and through those doors like I want to, I stand and wait. "Mr. Jameson?" he asks.

"That's me," I tell him.

"Right, well, your wife is in recovery."

His words sink in as I steady my breathing. "She's alive?" I don't know why I ask it, but I need to hear it. I need him to confirm.

"She is." He nods. "It was touch and go there for a bit. But we're optimistic. We still need to run some tests, but as it stands, there doesn't appear to be any permanent damage."

"I need to see her," I tell him.

"There's a limit of two visitors at a time." He glances at the crowd of friends and family currently surrounding me. I don't give a fuck about anyone else seeing her. I need to see her. "She's still asleep, but you can follow me."

"I'll come with you," my mom says while stepping up next to me. I nod in acknowledgement and we both follow the doctor.

I'm not prepared for this. I don't know if I ever could be as I walk over to the bed and see all the machines and wires attached to Montana's body. I focus on the one that shows me her heartbeat. As long as it's steady, everything else will be okay.

She's okay. She's going to get through this. We will get through this. Together. I reach out and pick up her hand. Her skin is cold. "Why is she so cold?" I ask my mom.

My mom touches the back of her hand to Montana's forehead. "She's okay, Luke. It's just the hospital's air-conditioning. Hospitals are always cold."

"She needs another blanket. Montana doesn't like being cold."

"I'll get her another blanket," Mom says. "Luke?"

I look up and wait for her to continue. "She is okay. She will be okay. But are you okay?"

"I feel like I've fucked up and I can't do anything to fix it. I have no control. I couldn't save her."

"Oh, baby, this isn't your fault. You didn't do this to her."

"I took her to that cemetery. I should have just brought her home." I shake my head. I'm not sure I'll ever forgive myself for this.

"I'm going to say this one more time, Luke Jameson. This isn't your fault. Don't let guilt eat you alive from the inside out, especially for something you didn't do. When she wakes up, she's going to need you to be there for her. You can't do that if you're stuck in your own head."

"Okay." I nod before looking down at my wife again. I promised to never let anyone hurt her and it's already happened.

How can I keep her safe? What do I have to do to make sure that nothing can touch her? Besides locking her inside a tower. Because I don't think she'd go along with that plan.

I don't know how much time has passed when I finally feel her hand move in mine. My head pops up from where it was resting on the edge of her bed. "Tanna?"

Her eyes peer back at mine. "L-Luke?" she questions, her voice sounding hoarse.

"Shh, don't talk. Let me get you some water." I stand from the chair, and my mom is already handing me a cup. I hold the straw to Montana's lips and wait for her to sip at the water. "I'm so sorry."

"Why?" she whispers. "What did you do?"

"I shouldn't have taken you there," I admit. "Do you remember what happened?"

"I saw Sean," she tells me.

I nod my head. "We were at the cemetery, and you were shot, Tanna."

"No, I saw him. I saw my brother, Luke," she repeats, a little more firmly this time.

I look over to my mom. "I'm going to go let the doctors know she's awake," Mom says. "But first, how are you feeling, Montana? Are you in pain?"

Montana shakes her head.

"Okay, I'll be back in a sec," Mom says.

Montana waits for my mom to leave the room before looking at me again. "Luke, I saw him. He was there."

"Where?"

"I don't know. But I saw him. He said to tell you to break away. No, that's not right. He said to tell you to... break out!"

"Break out? You sure that's what he said?" I ask her.

"Yes, I'm sure." She nods her head, adding, "And he didn't kill himself."

Okay, I'm not sure what drugs they're pumping her with but Montana is not making much sense. I saw Sean. Afterwards. I know he put a razor to his wrists.

"He said he was protecting me from something. And he mentioned our mother. I don't know what any of it means. But I do know he didn't choose to leave us."

I would love nothing more than to believe that. I wish it were true. I've gone through so many mixed feelings about my best friend's death. But I've never once considered he didn't do it to himself.

My mind goes back to what Montana said. A break out is when you get possession of the puck in your defensive end and move out of the zone to attack.

If any of this is true, what could Sean be trying to tell me?

And then it clicks when I remember a conversation I had with Sean in high school after getting into a fight at a party. Sean told me that I should break out, and then went on to explain how I needed to plan better when facing an opponent. He always related everything to hockey. He told me I needed to find their purpose first, their intent, then build up my defenses and finally attack. According to him, you can't fight if you don't know *why* you're fighting.

I need to find out why Andrew has his sights set on Montana, what his purpose is and what his interests are. I assumed he was an abusive asshole, a weak fucker who uses women as his punching bag. I never considered that maybe there's more to it than that.

What the fuck am I missing?

"I love you," Montana says, breaking me from my train of thought.

"I love you so much. I was so fucking scared I lost you." I lean in and press my lips to her forehead. And she offers me a weak smile.

"You can't get rid of me that easily, Luke Jameson."

Chapter Twenty-Nine

I was shot. Words I never expected to hear myself think, let alone say. And I saw my brother; although I'm not one hundred percent sure Luke believes me. I know I did, though. I'm certain of it.

Sean said he didn't choose to take his own life,

and I'm going to make it my mission to find out what happened. Why did he feel like he had to die to protect me? I can't think of any reason.

My heart hurts. I've hated Sean for so long for leaving me behind. But finding out that he did what he did *for me*? The guilt is too much. I wish he had spoken to me before he did it. Maybe we could have figured it out, worked out a better solution to whatever problem he had.

Then there's the fact he mentioned our mother. What could she have to do with any of this? I'm so confused. I have so many questions.

There's always the other scenario, the one where I didn't see my brother and it was all nothing more than a drug-induced dream.

I've been stuck in this hospital bed all week. I've had visitors, more visitors than I've ever had come to the hospital for me before. Of course, I didn't have friends back then. And I have Luke now... and new friends.

I'm itching to get out of here, though. I want to go home. To Luke's house. I want to get out of this town. The longer I'm here, the more chances Andrew has to find me. Luke says that he's the one who shot me. They have video footage of him entering and leaving the cemetery. At first, I didn't

Kylie Kent

believe it. Andrew liked to see my pain up close. He never used weapons on me, preferring to use his own hands to deliver the blows.

And then I saw him...

Except it wasn't really him. I don't know. It's hard to explain. It looked like him, but he had a completely different demeanor about him. He didn't look like the carefree bartender I first met. And he also didn't seem like the control freak of an abusive boyfriend I settled for. I watched the video footage five times before Luke took it away. I wish I could figure out what was different about the man on the screen. Why it was Andrew but also wasn't him. I just have that feeling in my gut.

"A little help would be great, Sean," I whisper. I love puzzles. I'm a mathematician—well, I want to be one anyway. I can solve nearly impossible equations, so why can't I solve this?

"We're breaking you out, Tanna," Luke says, walking into the room with Grayson, Liam and Travis behind him.

"I can go home?" I ask excitedly. I've been trying to get out of this place for days now.

"Yep, we're going home." Luke smiles at me before turning around to glare at his friends. "You all

252

need to get the fuck out so she can get dressed," he growls.

"We'll be outside." Grayson spins right back around, followed by the other two. When the door closes behind them, Luke steps to my bedside.

"I got Aliyah to pick up some clothes for you." He holds up the plastic bag.

"Thank you." I push myself to a sitting position while gritting my teeth. It still hurts, but I do my best to hide the pain. It's not like I don't have a lot of practice.

"Tanna, you don't have to pretend for me. I know it hurts. And I hate seeing you in pain. I would do literally anything if I could take your pain away for you. But I don't want you to think you need to pretend for me," Luke says, seeing right through my act.

"It's not that bad. I've had worse." I joke. Judging by the look on his face, it doesn't land well.

"Come on. I'll help you," Luke says, emptying the contents of the bag onto the bed.

By the time I'm dressed, I have to admit I'm winded and Luke has to practically hold me up as we walk to the door.

"You sure you don't want a chair?" he asks.

"I want to walk."

The moment we finally make it outside, I pause, clinging to Luke's shoulder while my eyes widen at the scene in front of us. There are ten really big SUVs lined up at the curb with men in suits standing beside each one. The middle vehicle has its door held open, like everyone is waiting for someone important to appear.

"Is someone famous here?" I whisper.

"You mean besides me, right? Hi, not sure we've met. Liam King. *The* Liam King." Aliyah's husband holds out his hand to me with a giant grin on his face.

I laugh but stop immediately when my stomach feels like it's going to rip open. "Ow, don't make me laugh." I curse at him under my breath.

"Ignore him, Tanna. We're driving back to Vancouver. Come on." Luke guides me over to the open door.

"Where did all these cars and people come from?" I ask him.

"Courtesy of the Monroe family." Luke shrugs, and I lower my voice.

"They're all mobsters?"

"They all work for Gray's dad," Luke says with a smirk. In other words, *yeah, they're all mobsters.*

"Okay." I climb into the car and Luke slides in after me.

"There isn't anything I won't do to protect you. I'm not letting what happened in the cemetery ever happen again." He picks up my hand, entwining our fingers as he rests our joined palms on his thigh.

"It's not your fault," I remind him for what feels like the thousandth time. All I get in response is a grunt.

As the car pulls away from the hospital, I lean my head on Luke's shoulder. The drive back to Vancouver is a few hours, so I might as well get as comfortable as I can. I close my eyes and work through deciphering the puzzle that is my life at the moment. The only conclusion I can come up with is the one where I have to find my mother. I need to know what Sean knew, why he felt like he had to protect me from her... Or was it from someone else?

I have no idea where to start, but maybe if I go through Sean's things, I might find something. The only problem is all of his things are at my father's house.

I lift my head and look up at Luke. "Do you think you can get those boxes from my dad's garage? The stuff you packed up from your college dorm? Sean's stuff?"

"I can ask him. What are you looking for?"

"I need to find my mother," I explain. "I don't

know what Sean uncovered when he tracked her down, and I know she doesn't deserve my efforts to find her when she's done nothing to find me. But I need to know. Something isn't right."

"Okay, I'll look into it." Luke kisses my forehead and pulls me back against his side.

"Thank you."

I could go to my dad's. He'd let me in. I'm sure of that. I just can't face him yet. I'm not ready to address that bag of emotions. It's something I need to try to work through with Dr. West first. Maybe then I can face it head-on.

I look down at my left hand, the gold band staring back at me. I'm married, and instead of basking in our marital bliss, Luke and I have been stuck in a hospital room all week.

"I'm going to buy you a better ring. With a huge diamond that aliens on Mars will be able to see and know that you're my wife." Luke brings my hand up to his mouth and kisses my ring finger.

"I don't want a new ring. I like this one," I tell him.

Chapter Thirty

The first thing I notice when we get home is the increased security Gray has arranged. He tried to convince me to bring Montana to his place. That we'd be better off staying together. I couldn't do that, though. He has a little girl to consider and whatever danger is chasing

Montana, well, I don't want it touching Gray's daughter. I need to be able to focus on my wife. I can't have distractions.

I called the team and asked for a timeout, so to speak. And let's just say that neither Coach nor Mr. Monroe was on board with that request. They have, however, agreed to let me bring Montana everywhere I go. It was either that, or I'd have to call my lawyer and find a way to pull out of my contract. I don't want to, but I'm not leaving her alone. Ever again if I can help it.

"Thanks for everything," I tell Gray, after I've tucked Montana into our bed, telling her I was going to get her a cup of hot chocolate and see our guests out.

"No need to thank me," he says.

"You'll call, yeah? If you guys find anything?" I ask. He and Vinny have been trying to track Andrew all week. We know it was him at the cemetery. The plates on the car he used were fakes, but the guys managed to track the car down to a town two hours north of Vancouver. Liliana also called in a favor with her father, who is the Don of one of the five families of New York.

We have two crime families looking for this fucker, and he's still in the wind. I'm finding it hard to believe that he's intelligent enough to keep hiding. He'll fuck up eventually, and when he does, we'll be ready to pounce. Until then, Montana is not leaving this house without a fucking convoy of protection around her.

"You'll be the first to know," Gray assures me.

I walk him out to the front door and then head into the kitchen. Where I turn the kettle on and pile a shit-ton of hot chocolate mix into a mug. Looking out the back window, I see three of the Monroe soldiers posted in the yard.

What would I do right now if I didn't have the connections I do? Would I run? Hire personal security?

I never thought I'd have to live under these conditions. I'm not Gray. I knew he's always had to take these insane precautions, surrounding himself with his father's men—even if you didn't see them, they were always there. He's not a made man. Not last I checked anyway. He very well could be now with what he did to the assholes who threatened his wife and daughter. Let's just say... he got a lot of practice with his stick skills. Either way, having the last name Monroe comes with the risks. And now, I guess so does the name Jameson.

I pull my phone out and find the number for

Montana's father. I should be calling to tell him that I married his daughter. That's not why I'm reaching out, though. I need to get Montana those boxes. I don't think she'll find whatever she's looking for, but I told her I'd get them so that's exactly what I plan to do. Pressing dial on his number, I wait for him to answer. I'm ready to hang up when the call finally connects.

"Luke?"

"Yeah, it's me. How are you, sir?" I ask him.

"I've seen better days. What can I do for you, Luke?"

"Sean's boxes. The ones I dropped off from our dorm. Do you still have them by any chance?"

"They're in the garage. I was hoping Montana would come by to go through them one day. But she... Well, what do you want them for?"

It's on the tip of my tongue to mention that Montana is here, with me. That she's my wife. I can't take that away from her, though. If she wants her father to know she got married, she will tell him. In her own time.

"I'm missing a trophy. I thought I might have packed it with Sean's stuff accidentally. You mind if I have a courier collect the boxes so I can go through them? I'll return everything when I'm done looking, of course."

"Ah, yeah, and you said you'll send them back though, right? Montana will want them one day." He sounds so hopeful. He hasn't given up on her yet.

"Yeah, I think she will too. I promise to send everything back."

"Okay. Is that all?" he asks.

"One more thing... what do you know about their mother? Sean mentioned something about finding his mother before he... well, before... Did you know?"

"Sean found his mother? Did he say where?" Mr. Baker sounds surprised and then a little concerned.

"No."

"I don't know where my wife ran off to, and it really doesn't make any difference now, does it? Sean's dead and Montana... she's better off not knowing anything about her mother."

Does he know the conditions Montana was living in? How could a father be okay with his daughter dating some asshole who beat on her? I can't imagine ever walking away and leaving someone I loved with someone like that. No matter how old they were. I'd drag my daughter out of that hellhole, right after I killed the bastard who laid his hands on her.

"Okay, thanks for your time, sir." I cut the call and pocket my phone. I'll organize a courier to collect the boxes tomorrow.

Mr. Baker's reaction to the mention of his ex-wife is surprising. It could also just be the fact he hasn't heard anyone ask about her in so long. I remember my mom was beside herself after Mrs. Baker left. Mom lost her best friend. She looked everywhere, tried to find her to talk some sense into her. She never did though. Wherever that woman went, the notes she sent telling us to stop looking made it clear she didn't want to be found.

By the time I rush back upstairs, Montana is asleep. I place the cup of hot chocolate on the bedside table and head for the shower. Leaving the door open just a crack. I want to be able to hear her if she wakes up. I thought maybe it was just the hospital setting that was affecting her sleep, but even after being shot, Montana hasn't had a nightmare since the night we were married. I'm hoping it's a positive sign, a step towards moving forward in her recovery.

After showering, I sit on the bed next to Montana, who is still sound asleep, and open my laptop. I plug in my headphones and load up this week's replay reels. I haven't been there, with my team, but I have to return to the ice tomorrow.

News of Montana's shooting was leaked to the press by someone in the hospital, which is why we're home now. I discharged her with the intention of having a doctor do house calls. But Liliana insisted on bringing in her family doctor and wouldn't take no for an answer. So, now, not only is my wife being protected by my friend's mob connections; she's also going to be treated by one of their doctors.

I never would have thought this would be my life. Up until I was drafted, I lived a very normal suburban existence. My parents had blue-collar jobs. I never wanted for anything, but we were far from wealthy. I know my parents sacrificed a lot and missed out on certain niceties in order for me to play hockey. It's not the cheapest sport to put your kid in. It's the reason I paid their mortgage off with my first official NHL paycheck.

Speaking of money, Montana needs her own bank accounts. I pause the video, open my emails, and fire off a message to my manager, requesting that he add Montana to all my accounts as well as open one solely in her name. I don't want her to think she ever has to be dependent on someone else again. Even if she wanted to leave me, I'd fucking let her take it all. I would never hold finances over her head. I never want to control her. To me, she is the most beautiful when she's living for herself, when she's happy and seems fulfilled.

I need to talk to her about what she wants to do... after she's recovered and we've found and eliminated Andrew. I'm not an idiot. I know she can't follow me around forever, no matter how much I'd love her to do just that.

She stirs next to me and I close my laptop. "Did I fall asleep?" she asks.

"You did," I tell her. "You don't have to wake up, babe."

"What are you doing?"

"Watching replays."

"Sounds... fun?" she says, though it comes out more like a question than an observation.

"It's my job, one I need to keep up with," I remind her. "I spoke with your dad by the way."

Her body freezes. "You did?"

"Mhmm, I'm getting a courier to collect Sean's boxes tomorrow."

"Did you tell him? About me? About us?"

"No. I didn't tell him that you're here, or that you're my wife. I honestly thought he might have brought it up himself. Seeing as it's been all over the news. But he didn't seem to know."

"He won't watch sports news. He hasn't since Sean... He won't even watch hockey anymore," she says.

"Well, whenever you're ready to tell him, I'll be there with you and we'll do it in person, but I'll fly him here. We are not going back home."

"I'm fine with never going back."

"If you could have any car in the world, what would you pick?" I ask, changing the subject to something lighter.

"You're not buying me a car, Luke. I don't need one. I don't even go anywhere," Montana says.

"I am buying you a car. You can either have a say in the type by telling me your dream car, or you can just be surprised. Either way, you're getting one. One day, you will want to go somewhere, Tanna. And when that day comes, I want you to have the means, the freedom to do so."

"I don't have a dream car," she says, then seems to consider her options for a moment. "I guess it's better if you just surprise me. But nothing flashy or over the top."

"Nothing flashy, got it." I smile, already knowing exactly what I'm getting her.

Chapter Thirty-One

I'm freezing. No matter how many layers I put on, I can't get warm enough. But I don't move. I stay rooted to my seat, watching Luke practice. Aliyah and Kathryn just left, mentioning something about taking Graycee shopping.

We've been home for three days. I went through

all of Sean's stuff from his dorm room yesterday. I couldn't find anything that would lead me to where my mother is. I don't know how he found her. Or why. I remember the note she left us back when we were kids, telling us not to look for her. That she didn't love us enough to stay. She didn't say those exact words, but the intent was there. If I had money, I'd hire a private investigator to find her. I need to know what Sean knew, and if he wasn't responsible for taking his own life, I want to know who made him do it. Why he felt like he had to do it to protect me.

A body fills the seat next to mine and then there's a blanket dangling in front of me. "You look like you're freezing," Liliana says.

"I am. How are you not?" I ask while eyeing the dress she's wearing.

"I like the cold. Plus, I just take one look at Travis out there on the ice, his muscles flexing and bulking..." She smirks. "...and my entire body heats up."

"Gross. Never say that shit again," a voice says from behind us. I turn around, expecting to see Liliana's cousin Enzo. It's not him, but it is someone from her family. The resemblance is too uncanny for it not to be. But this guy looks like he should be in school. He's young. "Hi, I'm Dante." The kid holds out a palm towards me.

"Montana." I smile, glancing at his hand before accepting the gesture.

"I'm her cousin, the best one," he says as he drops his arm back to his side, turns to Liliana, and scrunches up his face. "Tell me again why we're freezing our asses off to watch these guys practice?"

"Because I want to, and Pops says you have to follow me everywhere." Liliana shrugs.

"You really never go anywhere alone?" I ask her.

"I do. But my dad's being overly cautious right now. He gets like this after a shooting. His paranoia will wear off in a few months."

"That's nice, though. That he loves you enough to worry," I tell her. Not all of us have that.

"I know," Liliana says.

"Lil, you got any gum?" Dante asks, leaning forward and wrapping his arms around the back of her chair.

"In here." Liliana passes him her handbag without taking her eyes off the ice. "Don't interrupt me. This is the best part."

She's not wrong. Watching these guys stretch is something else.

"Again, gross," Dante grumbles while digging

through her bag. A couple of seconds later, he grunts. "What the fuck is this, Lil?"

We both turn around to look at him, and then at the pink handgun he's pinching between his fingers like the girliness might be contagious. It's... bedazzled with jewels.

"Isn't it pretty?" Liliana smiles. "Travis got it for me in Vegas."

"He couldn't have gotten you a Rolex or something? You don't need a gun, Liliana." Dante scowls at her.

"Actually, I do. Everyone else in the family has one, and it's not like I don't know how to use it." She snatches the weapon out of his hands and drops it back into her bag.

"I'm telling Zio Theo," he says.

"Go ahead. My dad won't care," Liliana counters. Even I can tell she doesn't believe her own words and I haven't known her that long.

I return my focus to the ice. I don't need to be involved in whatever family drama these two have. I also feel like the less I know about Liliana's family, the better.

"How are you feeling? Really?" she asks me.

"I'm okay," I tell her. "It's better every day." I

downplay how much pain I'm in. Again. Something I'm well versed in doing.

"How's the doc been treating you?"

"Like I'm royalty." I laugh. The Valentino family doctor makes daily house calls. I'm not sure why, but he treats me as if *his* life depends on me keeping *mine*.

"Good. I'm glad I could do something to help. You know, if you need anything else, all you have to do is ask."

"I know, and I appreciate that. I really do," I tell her. And then a thought comes to mind. "Actually, now that you mention it... Say I were looking for someone who's been gone a really long time, how would one go about finding them?"

"We have people for that. Trackers," Dante chimes in, clearly listening in on our conversation.

"And where would someone find these trackers?" I ask him, looking back over my shoulder. "If someone needed to hire them, I mean..."

"Someone doesn't. *Someone* gives me a name and I pass it on to them," he says.

"Just like that? Just a name?"

"Yep, just like that. Who are you looking for?"

"That obvious, huh?" I chew on my bottom lip, and Dante lifts a brow as if to say: *really?* "My mother, but I'm not even sure where to start looking," I admit. Then go on to explain how she left when I was young and that I believe my brother might have found her before he died.

"What's her name?" Dante asks.

"Kristy Baker," I tell him, then quickly add, "But I don't want you to call your tracker. It's okay."

"I'll let you know when they've found something," he says, ignoring my attempt to backpedal. I shouldn't be asking for his help.

Wait... Did I ask for his help? I don't think I actually did.

I pull out my journal as I wait for Luke to come out of the locker room. I'm as alone as I can be in this hallway with two burly men in black-on-black suits posted at each end. They've been following me around everywhere. Honestly, I appreciate that they are.

I'd be lying if I said I wasn't a little freaked out after being shot. Someone actually tried to kill me. *Andrew* tried to kill me. There's that little voice in the back of my head telling me that it wasn't him; although I know it was. I mean, it looked like him in that video footage.

There's probably a messed-up part of my brain that wants to believe that he wouldn't have ever gone that far. I know it's stupid, and I'm sure it's part of the reason I stayed with him for as long as I did. I always wanted to believe that he would get better. I can't say that I loved him exactly. I did care for him, though. At least at the start.

But love? I could never love anyone because my heart has always belonged to Luke Jameson.

Dear Sean,

I'm scared. I have no idea if I really did see you or not, but I'm glad I saw whatever it was that I saw. I needed it. I needed you.

I still need you, but I don't hate you anymore. I'm trying really hard to figure out the puzzle you've left me with, though. A little guidance on where to start would be great, by the way!

I'd like to believe that you're up there somewhere. I don't know why you couldn't help me when I asked years ago, but if you have any kind of pull on those heavenly strings, I could use a favor.

I need to know. I can't live in fear forever. I need to know that Andrew isn't going to keep coming after me until he succeeds in killing me. I was shot, but you know that already.

I'm not ready to die, Sean. I have so much to live for now. I want to live. I want that life I dreamed about. The life with Luke.

The nightmares have stopped. It's weird. After I married Luke, they just stopped. I keep waiting for them to come back. But each morning after I wake up, I'm surprised when they're not there.

Anyway, like I said, please send me some guidance.

XX,
Montana

Chapter Thirty-Two

The shrill ringtone of my phone wakes me. Swiping out an arm, I fumble for the device and see Gray's number on the screen. And then notice it's three in the morning.

"Yeah," I answer.

"We got him. Get dressed. I'm coming to get you."

His words have a sobering effect. I'm wide awake now. "You got him?" I ask, pulling the covers off.

"Yeah, Vinny's got your package ready for collection," Gray says cryptically.

"Okay, I'll meet you out front." I look back at the bed. Montana is still sleeping. "Shit," I hiss under my breath. "I can't leave Montana alone, Gray."

I know that *technically* she's not alone. There are a shit-ton of security guys posted around the property. No one is getting in. I just don't want her to wake up and find me gone. I'm also not about to wake her up and be forced to answer questions about where I'm going.

"Already on it. Kathryn called Aliyah. She's on her way to your place with Lil and O'Neil."

"Thanks." I run a hand through my hair. "For everything, Grayson. I don't know how I'd get through all this shit without you."

"Don't get soft on me now, Jameson. We're family. This is what family does for each other. I'll meet you out front in ten," he says, then cuts the call.

I pull out a pair of jeans and a hoodie, throw them on, and shove my feet into my runners. When I walk back into the bedroom, I pull the blankets up over Montana's body. "I'm going to make your demons disappear," I whisper before slipping out the door.

The moment I make it down the stairs, I hear a commotion in the kitchen.

"When did your brother call you?" I ask Aliyah when I see everyone crowded around my kitchen.

"About twenty minutes ago. What's going on? All he said was I had to come over here." She raises a questioning brow at me.

"I... ah... I have to go do something. I didn't want Montana to wake up and find me gone."

"Okay, well, we're all here, so you go do what ya gotta do." Aliyah doesn't pry any further. She and Liliana grew up in a world where the less you know, the better.

"Thanks. Sorry for dragging you all out of bed."

"Are you kidding? I'm raiding your snacks, bro. My wife doesn't let me have the good stuff. Yours hasn't taken over the pantries yet," King says, moving from one cabinet to the next.

Liliana walks up to me. "Be careful. Don't do anything that means you won't be coming home to her, because I don't want to see that girl go through any more pain."

"I'll be careful," I tell her.

"You know you don't need to do anything, right? You don't have to have that kind of shit on your conscience," Gray says. "There's nothing wrong with letting someone else take care of a problem for you."

"How's your conscience?" I ask him. We both know what I mean.

"Fine." He shrugs.

"I need to do this. I feel it in my bones. I want his fucking head ripped off his shoulders. He shot my wife, Gray."

"I know. Come on then. Let's go."

I follow him into the abandoned building and hear the groans as soon as we enter. I smile while wondering how loud I can make this fucker scream. Gray leads us into a large open room, where his brother and a few other guys are sitting at a makeshift table playing poker. That's not what has my attention, though. No, all my focus is on the guy sitting on a wooden chair in the middle of the space. He looks right at me and smiles. Fucking smiles.

"I've been waiting for you to show up," he says.

"Yeah? Why's that?" I take a step and then

another, but before I reach him, Gray's brother is standing next to me. Pointing a gun at the fucker's temple. "Andrew? Right? This has been a long time coming." My right fist slams into the side of his head, knocking him and the chair to the ground.

He laughs. And then, like a goddamn ninja, he jumps to his feet, his wrists free of his restraints and Vinny's gun in his hand. I blink.

What the fuck just happened?

He's not aiming at me, though. No, his focus is on Gray's brother. Shit. Without a word, a gunshot sounds out and the weapon that was in Andrew's hand clatters against the cement floor.

I look to my right. To Gray and the gun clutched in his grip. Where that came from, I have no idea.

"Thanks, bro." Vinny smiles at Gray before kicking a leg out and knocking Andrew back onto his ass. "Fancy yourself a ninja, do ya?" Vinny asks, as if reading my mind.

"You have no idea." Andrew laughs again.

"I know you shot my wife after you spent years beating on her. You know what kind of man beats a woman?" I ask him. "A weak piece of shit undeserving of his next breath."

"I shot her, but I'm not who you think I am. Andrew was supposed to finish the job. He failed, so

I had to pick up the pieces. You think I'll be the last? I won't be. You can't save her. It's her destiny."

I have no idea what the fuck this guy's talking about. And right now, I don't fucking care. I jump on top of him, my vision red as I throw my fist into his head over and over again. I don't know how long I'm on him before I'm pulled off.

"That's enough, Luke. He's done," Gray says.

I look down at the bloodied mess on the floor, then drop my foot on his head one more time. "It's not enough. He needs to feel what he did to her," I grind out while my chest heaves.

"I know. But dead men can't feel shit," he says.

I stare at the body and then at my hands. I killed him. I actually killed him. I try to dig into my soul for some hint of remorse. I don't find it.

"Guys, you might want to look at this," Vinny says while holding up a wallet. He reaches in, pulls something out, and hands it to me.

It's a photo of Andrew... and Andrew? There are two of him. "What the fuck? He has a twin? There's another one of him out there?" I look back down at what's left of the fucker on the floor, and then his words come back to me. "Who was he talking about? When he said they're going to keep coming for her?" I ask aloud to no one in particular.

"No idea, but I'll find out," Vinny assures me.

"Where did you find him?"

"Tracked him down to a shitty little house a few hours from here. No one else was there."

"Send some guys. Have them search the place. If this other fucker is out there, I want him found," Gray adds while tapping on the photo.

"Montana was insistent that it wasn't Andrew at the cemetery. And I think she was right. That's not him." I gesture to the body.

"If this Andrew fuckwit is still out there, I'll find him, Luke. Go home—but wash up first. Your new bride doesn't need to see you like this." He nods to the blood covering my face, chest, and hands.

"Thank you." I don't know how to express just how grateful I am to the Monroe family. I know Vinny's only doing this for his brother, but I'm still fucking glad to have his help.

Chapter Thirty-Three

I roll over and reach out for Luke. The stitches in my stomach pull, slowing my movements. When my hand lands on cold sheets, I open my eyes. He's not here. He's always here when I wake up. I listen for a few moments, thinking maybe he's in the bathroom. But he's not in there either.

Where is he?

I pull myself out of bed. My body is still a little achy first thing in the morning. Usually, the pain eases a bit once I start moving around more. I grab my robe from the hook on the back of the bathroom door and make my way downstairs.

I hear them when I reach the top landing. The voices. Aliyah and Liliana. How long have I been asleep? When I look outside, I see the sun is only just rising. It's early, and they're here. Something isn't right.

I turn around, quietly shutting myself back in the bedroom. Whatever has them here, it can't be good. No one just drops by someone's house at this hour because they have good news to share.

Where is Luke? Is he downstairs with them?

I can't hear any more bad news right now. I don't want to. Especially if it's about Luke. Oh god, what if something's happened to him? What if Andrew found him?

I pick up my phone from the bedside table, find Luke's number, and dial. "Tanna, you okay?" he asks as soon as the call connects.

"I... ah... I woke up and you... Why are Aliyah and Liliana in your house?"

"I had to run an errand. I'm on my way back

now. I didn't want you to wake up alone so the girls came over," he tells me.

"You're okay though, right? There's nothing wrong with you?"

"I'm fine. Promise. I'll be home in fifteen minutes. Where are you?"

"In the bedroom," I say.

"Okay. You didn't go downstairs?"

"I didn't want to see anyone. I thought... Last time I woke up this early to people in my house was when Sean died... I thought that something happened to you," I admit.

"Shit, I'm sorry, Tanna. I didn't think... Fuck, I'm sorry I didn't think. But I'm fine. Promise."

"It's stupid. I know that. I just can't imagine losing you. I love you," I say, clutching the phone like a lifeline.

"I love you too. I'm picking up breakfast. If you see Liam, tell him to stop eating my snacks."

"Okay." I laugh. Luke is very serious about his food. He always has been. "I'll see you soon."

Luke hangs up and I get dressed in a pair of yoga pants and a sweater, brushing the tangles out of my hair before I head downstairs. I find Aliyah and Liliana in the living room with their husbands.

"Morning."

"Good morning. How'd you sleep?" Aliyah asks from her spot on the sofa.

"Good. I'm sorry Luke had you all come over here." I feel slightly embarrassed as I twist the hem of my shirt.

"Oh, it's fine. Don't worry about it." Liliana smiles at me.

"He's on his way home with breakfast." I lower myself onto the sofa before landing my glare on Liam, who's currently shoving a handful of chips into his mouth. "And he said to tell you to stop eating his snacks."

"But he gets all the good stuff." Liam pouts.

Aliyah rolls her eyes. "You don't need all that sugar in your life, Liam King. You need to stay in shape if you're gonna be my meal ticket to an early retirement."

"You own a hockey team, Aliyah. You can retire whenever you want," Liam reminds her.

"My father owns a hockey team. Not me. *I* own a Liam King." She smiles wide, and I watch as Liam leans in and kisses her.

"Yes, you do."

"Okay, well, you can eat whatever you want then, I guess. I'll just order more." I laugh. And then it hits me. I've never done a single bit of grocery shopping since I arrived. I haven't cooked, and I've barely cleaned anything. I'm the world's shittiest houseguest.

I need to do better. I'm not a houseguest anymore. I'm his wife. I wonder what he expects of me in this new role. We haven't really discussed anything. I don't know if I should be picking up groceries. I don't even know where the grocery store is located. Or how to get there...

"Does anyone know where Luke buys his groceries?" I ask aloud.

Travis is the one who laughs this time. "He doesn't. Aliyah orders it all for him."

"You do?" My eyebrows knit in confusion.

"I've done it for years. But I haven't ordered anything in weeks. He's been doing it himself," she says.

I've been waiting for everyone to leave. Luke and Grayson turned up with breakfast; Kathryn and

Graycee came over as well. It's nice to be surrounded by Luke's friends. I guess they're *my* friends now too. But one look at his face and I wanted to ask him where he went. What he did.

Then I saw his hands and my stomach dropped. I grew up with a brother who got into as many fights as he played hockey games. I know what it looks like when your fists have been hitting something... or someone. And right now, Luke's knuckles are swollen and raw.

As soon as the door closes and Aliyah and Liam are safely on the other side, I head upstairs. I want to ask Luke what happened. I just don't know how. What if it's none of my business and he gets angry that I'm prying into his life?

"I ask the questions, bitch." A palm lands across my cheek with a loud slap. At least it's open-handed this time. It hurts worse when it's a closed fist.

"I'm sorry. I didn't mean to," I plead. *"How about I make you your favorite pasta?"* As I go to step

around him, towards the kitchen, I'm pulled back by my hair.

"I don't think you're sorry enough yet," Andrew sneers into my face, his saliva splattering across my cheek.

"I am, Andrew. I'm sorry," I insist, while trying to wiggle out of his hold.

His grip on my hair tightens as he pushes me up against the wall before his free hand wraps around my throat. "I should squash your vocal cords. Maybe then I won't have to hear your annoying fucking voice, Montana," he says as he gradually presses down on my neck.

My head shakes from side to side as much as it can. Tears stream down my face, and I try to speak but I can't get the words out.

Andrew chuckles. "That's better. That's how I like to hear you. Just like that. Nothing."

"Montana, open your eyes."

I look around the room for Luke. I recognize his voice. How is he here? He wasn't here. Andrew was.

"Tanna, open your eyes. You're okay. I've got you," Luke says.

I blink, and then it's Luke's face in front of me. Not Andrew's. I push myself back, away from him, and scan the room.

Where is he? Andrew's here. I know he is. Except, when I take in my environment, I see that it's not the shitty little apartment I used to share with my ex. This is Luke's house. I'm on the second floor landing with my back pressed up against the wall.

"Tanna, it's okay. I'm not going to hurt you," Luke says while slowly reaching out to me. I don't move away from his touch this time. Instead, I jump on him, wrapping my body around his.

"Don't let me go," I whisper. "Please, don't let me go."

"Never. I'm going to hold you forever and ever, Tanna," Luke promises. He's moving, but I don't open my eyes. I keep my face buried in his neck. My arms tighten around him when I feel him sit down. I can't let go. His hands run up and down my back. "Shh, it's okay. I've got you."

I can't stop crying. I haven't had one of these memories for a while. And I guess this one's made me realize I'm never going to escape them. I'm never going to escape what Andrew did to me. What I let him do to me. That's the worst part really. The guilt. Feeling like I *let* him. Because I stayed, time after time.

What's wrong with me that I'd let someone treat me that way? Am I that desperate to be loved?

Chapter Thirty-Four

I followed Montana upstairs and found her on the top landing with her body flush against the wall. Her eyes were closed and she was screaming, saying she was sorry over and over again.

I hope that Gray's brother finds the fucker alive. Andrew. If that was his twin I killed today, then that means I get to kill the sick son of a bitch all over again. And I fucking want to.

I'm holding my wife in my arms while she clings to me as if I'm the only thing keeping her together. I'll sit right here holding her for as long as she needs me to do it. I'm not going anywhere. "I'm always going to love you, Tanna. I'm sorry I can't make it all go away for you," I tell her.

"You... I love you," she says through choked sobs. "I'm sorry."

"No. Don't say that to me. You have nothing to apologize for."

"I'm sorry that I'm so broken. You deserve a better wife than what's left of me."

"There is absolutely nothing wrong with you. There is nothing that you ever have to apologize for. You are not broken, Montana. You are the picture-perfect, beautiful soul I've known and loved forever. You, Mrs. Jameson, are fucking amazing. I want you, all of you, the good and the bad. This, us, it's real, Tanna. There isn't a single bit of you that I'm not in love with."

We sit quietly for at least thirty minutes before Montana picks up her head. Her tears have slowed and eventually stop. I bring my thumbs up and wipe the wetness from her cheeks.

"It breaks my heart that I can't take away all of your pain," I whisper.

Montana stares at my hands. She doesn't say a word.

"What brought this on? Did I say something? Do something?"

She shakes her head. "I was going to ask you something... and then." She pauses, then adds, "I'm not supposed to ask, because it's none of my business."

"I'm your husband, Montana. That makes everything I do your business. There isn't anything you can't ask me. I will always tell you."

"You won't get mad?"

"There isn't enough anger I could ever feel that would make me hurt you. I will never do that to you, Tanna." I know I've said it before. I also know that she believes it. Sometimes I think she needs to hear it again, though.

"Where did you go? Why do your hands look like you've been hitting something?" She glances at my fists before peering up at me again.

"Gray called me this morning. His brother found Andrew."

At the mention of his name, Montana's eyes widen.

"Except, now, we're not so sure that guy was Andrew. We found this in his wallet." I pull the picture out of my pocket, even though it's the last thing I want to do. I don't want her to ever have to see this fucker's face again. The face of her abuser.

"There're two of him?" she gasps.

"Did you know he was a twin?" I ask her.

"No, he told me he was an only child. That his parents died when he was a kid."

It doesn't surprise me that the asshole lied to her. "I want to run away. I want to take you away from here. Somewhere no one will ever be able to find us," I admit.

"I've had this dream," she tells me.

"Oh yeah? What's in this dream?"

"You. You're skating with a little girl, our little girl." She smiles at me. "And then you have our son in your arms. I want that dream to become our reality, Luke. We can't run away just because things are... hard right now. It's going to get better."

"I want that dream too," I tell her.

"What happened to him? Andrew or was it his twin?"

"I... I made sure that whoever it was could never hurt you again."

"I'm sorry you had to do that."

293

"I'm not." And I mean that. I'd do it all over again and I will. Just as soon as we find his brother. "How about we do something fun?" I say, attempting to change the subject.

"Fun? Like what?"

"I have an idea. Come on." I push up from the bed and place Montana's feet on the ground. Then I take her hand in mine and lead her downstairs and into the garage.

"Where are we going? Shouldn't I get changed or something?" Montana asks.

"You look beautiful. You don't need to change for what we're doing." I open the passenger door of my Rover and wait for her to jump inside before sliding into the driver's seat. Then I turn on the ignition and look over to Montana. She really is the most beautiful person in the world. And she's my wife. I will never stop being thankful for that.

An hour later, I pull the car into a lot. "Where are we?" Montana asks, looking out the windshield.

"Shannon Falls. I used to come here a lot when I first moved to Vancouver." I climb out of the car and Montana is already stepping down by the time I reach her.

Taking her hand in mine, I lead her over to the walking track. Once we're on the platform, I guide her to sit down. It's surprisingly quiet here. It's a major tourist spot, but today we're practically the only ones here. The water cascades down in front of us.

"I used to come here to quiet the noise in my head," I say. "I would sit and think about the good times, with Sean, with you." I wrap my arm around her waist and kiss her temple. "We have a lifetime of great memories ahead of us, Tanna."

"We do," she agrees.

"What's your favorite moment in time?" I ask her.

"The day I married you." Montana smiles at me.

"Huh, mine too. But before that, what's your favorite memory of Sean?"

"It's... embarrassing." She shakes her head and stares at her shoes.

"I doubt that. Tell me anyway," I encourage her.

"When I got my period, I didn't have a mom anymore. Girls are supposed to have a mom to talk to about that sort of thing. Dad didn't know what to do. But Sean... He went to the store. He got me everything I needed. He talked to me about it and didn't make me feel weird, you know? Like I said, it's embarrassing."

"I remember that." Sean called me in a panic,

and I was the one who told him what he needed to do. What to say to her. I'm not going to tell her that, though. I'm not taking that memory of her brother away from her. Because the important thing is he did it. He went to the store. He bought her the things she needed and he spent hours talking to her that day.

"How do you remember?" Montana asks.

"I called him, to hang out, and he blew me off." I shrug.

"I think Sean was the only person who loved me. My entire life, he was the one person I knew would love me no matter what. And then, when he left, I was just... alone."

I fucking hate myself for leaving her after Sean died. I wanted to be there for her. I just didn't want to break the promise I made to my best friend. I didn't want to tarnish his memory by going after his little sister. I should never have made that stupid promise in the first place. I was sixteen when I made it. I think Sean always knew I had a thing for Tanna. He made damn sure I never acted on it, though.

But I can't dwell on the past anymore. This place. This is where I come to remember the good, not the bad.

"You know, when the bad memories get a hold of

you, try to think about the good times," I tell Montana. "I'm not saying it'll help, but it might."

"I thought they went away. I haven't had a nightmare or a memory like that in a while, and I just... I guess I hoped I was fixed," she says. "Today made me realize I'm probably never going to be fixed."

"You can't be fixed, Montana. Because like I said before and will repeat until you believe it too, you're not broken."

"I don't even know where the grocery store is, Luke. I don't know where to buy your snacks and I think Liam actually did eat them all." She looks as if she's put a lot of thought into this.

"It's okay. It's not that serious, Tanna. I can buy more snacks."

"But I'm your wife. I'm supposed to do things like that."

"Buy me snacks?" I raise an eyebrow at her. "I'm pretty sure, as my wife, you're supposed to *be* my snack."

Her face heats up and red creeps its way along her neck. "I... I want to do stuff. I just don't know what I'm supposed to do."

"You want to go grocery shopping? Let's go. I'll take you right now," I tell her.

"Can you even go into a store without being recognized?

"I can." I push to my feet, hold out a hand, and help Montana stand. I flinch when I see the twinge of pain on her face. "Fuck, I shouldn't have made you sit on the ground," I tell her.

"It's okay. I'm fine. Let's go replace your snacks. I know how you get when your hangry, and nobody needs that monster around." She laughs.

"But I have a never-ending supply of my favorite snack right now, so I'm good."

"A never-ending supply?"

"You, Montana. You're my favorite snack," I remind her.

"Well, you know... if you want, we can skip shopping and just go home? Maybe... *snack* in bed?"

My eyes rake up and down her body. I would love nothing more than to slam my dick inside her. But I can't. Not when she has a stomach full of stitches.

"I have a better idea." I grin as I take Montana's hand and lead her back to the car.

Chapter Thirty-Five

Luke opens the back door. "Hop in and lie down," he tells me. I give him a skeptical look, but do what he says. He climbs in after me and closes the door behind him.

"What are we doing?" I ask.

"I'm hungry and don't want to wait for a snack. I

can't fuck you right now, Tanna, but I can do something... *if* you promise to stay still. You can't move around and hurt yourself." His hands are already pulling my tights down my legs. He takes one foot out and then spreads my thighs open.

"Here? Luke, anyone could see." I try to close my legs.

"The windows are far too dark for anyone to see inside, and there's no one here. Just you and me, Tanna." His finger runs up the center of my folds, and an involuntary moan leaves my mouth. "Do you want me to make you feel good?" he asks. "Do you want me to lick this pussy until I wring every bit of pleasure from your body?"

I nod my head. I can feel myself get wetter at his words. Luke bends forward. His hands hold my thighs, keeping me spread wide open for him. Before I can protest, his tongue swipes through the center of my pussy. From bottom to top. My body lifts, and Luke's head pops up.

"Keep still or I'll have to stop," he warns.

I nod and bite down on my lip. There's no way I can keep still, but I'm going to try. I want this. Luke's tongue swipes up through my folds again, swirling around my clit before he closes his mouth over the hard bud, and he sucks. My hand flies up to my mouth, muffling the scream of pleasure coming out of me. Just when I think he can't possibly make me feel any better, Luke pushes a finger into my entrance and starts fucking me with his hand while sucking on my clit at the same time.

How the hell does he expect me to stay still right now?

My free hand grips the back of his head. I don't know if I'm pulling him closer towards me or trying to pull him off me. The sensations running through my body are almost too much to handle. I feel his teeth graze over my clit and then he's pushing another finger inside me.

"Oh God! Luke," I moan out.

He pumps those fingers in and out a few times. Then I feel my entire body tighten. My stomach hurts, but no way am I stopping this. I can feel the orgasm. It's there, just waiting for me to reach out and catch it. And I do.

I twist my fingers in Luke's hair as I hold his face over my pussy, grinding up into his mouth as I come. My legs shake with the force of the aftershocks, and then my entire body slumps back against the leather seat of his car. I'm totally spent. I didn't realize just how much I needed that. Luke continues to lick me until I can't handle the sensations anymore and I have to pull him off me.

"Favorite snack ever," he says with a smirk.

"I guess it's a good thing you have that never-ending supply then, huh?"

"Thank fuck." Luke's eyes glaze over my body. "Are you okay? Did I hurt you?"

"No, I'm good," I tell him. When he doesn't look like he believes me, I take his face in my hands. "I promise."

"Okay." He puts my foot back through the one leg hole of my panties and then my tights and drags the fabric up my thighs again. "You good?"

"I am, but are you?" I glance down at his crotch.

"I'll be fine. I've been dealing with a hard cock around you since I was sixteen." He laughs.

"I never noticed."

"Because I got good at hiding it," he says.

We never made it to the supermarket. Luke decided I'd worn myself out enough for today and should be resting. I tried to argue that I was fine, but really I'm glad to be curled up on the sofa next to him right now, and not out at the shops. This is my favorite place to be, when it's just him and me in our bubble. A bubble no one can pop.

Luke's phone rings. He ignores it but I notice the name on the screen.

"It's Liliana. You should answer it," I tell him.

He squints at the phone and then leans forward to pick it up. "Lil, what's up?" I don't hear what she says but he holds the phone to me. "It's for you."

I take it out of his hand. "Hello?"

"Hey, I tried your phone first, but it kept ringing out," Liliana says.

"Sorry. I left it upstairs. Is everything okay?" I ask, my eyebrows drawn down in concern. She doesn't usually call me.

"Yeah, I have some information for you. Is it okay if I pop over?"

"Of course," I say and then look at Luke. "Wait. Hold on a sec." I cover the receiver with my hand. "Liliana wants to come over. Is that okay?"

"Tanna, it's your house. If you want her to come over, then have her over," Luke says.

"Thank you." I uncover the phone. "Yes, it's okay," I tell Liliana.

"Great, because I'm at your front door now," she says and then the doorbell rings.

The phone cuts off and I set it back down on the table. "I'll get the door. Stay here," Luke says, kissing the top of my head as he gets up off the sofa.

A few minutes later, Luke walks back into the living room, followed by Liliana, Travis, and two of her cousins. Enzo and Dante. My brows knit together. I didn't realize they were all coming with her.

"Hey." I sit up straighter.

"Sorry to barge in, but I thought you'd want to see this," Liliana says before handing me a manilla folder.

"What is it?" I question while taking the folder.

"It's a dossier on Kristy Baker," Enzo answers for her.

"Her mother?" Luke lowers himself down next to me. He looks at the folder like he wants to tear it out of my hands. He doesn't though.

"It's... um... It might not be what you're expecting, Montana," Dante says.

"Why?" I'm already opening the file, sifting through the numerous pages of information and photos. Pictures of my mom. I haven't seen her in years, but I'd recognize her anywhere. You never forget the face of the woman who abandoned you.

Then I notice her clothes. "What's she wearing?" I flip through the photos. "And what is she doing?"

"She married Brenton Glenn, the leader of the Brent Brothers Brethren." Enzo sits down on the sofa in front of me.

I look up at him, confused. "What's the Brent Brothers Brethren?"

"It's a cult," he says. "Not your average *I'm going to be a hippie and get stoned every day* kind of cult either."

"What?" I look at Luke and quickly hand him the folder. I don't want to read it. "Why would my brother tell me not to look for her?"

"Because I bet he found out what she was planning. What they were planning," Dante says.

"What was she planning?" Luke chimes in, picking up my hand and covering it with his.

"Ah, it's not... Well, there's no easy way to say it."

I can see the pity in Enzo's eyes and I don't like it.

"She was going to sacrifice you for *the cause*," he says, putting extra emphasis on the last words.

"Sacrifice me? How?" I ask him.

"A blood ritual. The youngest child from each of

the leaders is supposed to be sacrificed in some ritual. They believe it will give them eternal life or some bullshit."

"How do you know this?"

"We went to the house with some of the Monroe men—the one where we found Andrew or rather his twin," Dante explains. "I found a laptop there. And, well, there's not much I can't hack into when it comes to computers. I managed to get into Adam's emails."

"Adam? Who's Adam?" I feel like my head is spinning.

"Andrew's twin, also the son of your mother's new husband," Enzo says.

I shake my head. "I don't know how... I don't get it. Why wouldn't Andrew tell me that?"

"From what I read, Andrew was supposed to collect you and bring you to the farm. You were both supposed to be sacrificed. I guess he got cold feet. Decided to keep you for himself and hid you away instead." Dante shrugs. "It's all in the email printouts I included in the file, exchanges between Adam and his father."

"My mom?" I look at Luke. "My mother wants to kill me?"

"That's not going to happen," Luke grinds out.

Then he turns his attention to Liliana's cousins. "Where is she? Montana's mother?"

"On a farm, about four hours west," Enzo replies. "We found something else, at that property." He looks at me and then at Luke. "Andrew's body was shoved into a deep freezer, his blood drained and stored in bags around him."

"Andrew's dead?" I choke on my words.

"He is."

"Okay." I nod.

That's good, right? He can't come for me now. He can't hurt me anymore. I thought I would feel something the moment I heard he was dead. I thought I'd feel more... free. But I'm not free, am I? I won't be free until this entire nightmare is over.

However, it does make sense. Why Sean was warning me to stay away from our mother. "Why would Sean have killed himself?" I ask Luke. "What am I missing?"

"We don't know, but I'd hazard a guess that he thought if he offered himself up, you'd be spared? Maybe," Dante suggests.

Chapter Thirty-Six

Montana hasn't said much. It's a lot to take in, I'm sure. It's not every day you find out your mother is planning to sacrifice your life for her cult. No one ever really knew what happened to Mrs. Baker, where or why she left. Just that it had to do with some new boyfriend. I guess, when you're living in a cult off the grid, it's easy to stay hidden. The woman I knew as a child never would have sacrificed her children, though. Then again, the woman I knew never would have left them either.

"How are you feeling?" I ask Montana, handing her a cup of tea.

"Thanks. I'm... I don't know how I feel," she says. "How do *you* feel?"

"Me? Besides the fact I want to find your mother and tear her limb from limb, see how she feels about being a goddamn fucking sacrifice?"

"Yeah, besides that." Montana sighs.

"I'm scared. I'm worried about you." I run a hand through my hair. "You know this is not a reflection of you, what your mother is trying to do."

I know Montana. She takes things personally, and the fact that her mother wants to kill her means she's going to think either she did something wrong or that if her own mother can't love her, then why would anybody else?

"I don't know," Montana says. "Why wouldn't Sean just tell me?"

"Sean would have wanted to protect you no

matter the cost, Tanna. He loved you." I cup her cheek in my hand. "*I* love you." I lean in and press my lips to hers.

"I love you too. But this is a lot, Luke. You didn't sign up for this level of crazy when you married me."

"What I signed up for was a lifetime with the most beautiful, the most kind, the most amazing woman I've ever known. And I already told you there are no take backs, Tanna. I'm keeping you as long as I possibly can. This life and the next, remember?"

"I remember. I just don't want you to feel like you have to be stuck with all... *this*."

"I'm not stuck. I love you, and I will put an end to this cult bullshit. Before the week is up. I promise." I will do whatever it takes to make sure Kristy Baker isn't a threat to my wife's life.

I can't imagine how Montana must feel. I know it's weighing on her more than she's letting on. I remember when Mrs. Baker left. Both Sean and Montana took it really hard. But it was Montana who cried for two weeks straight. Until one day, she just started acting like nothing happened.

"We're going to go there. To the farm. I'm going to put a stop to it all, Tanna," I tell her.

Montana shakes her head. "We should just call the police. Let them deal with it," she says.

"We can't do that." I cup her face in my hands and press my lips to the center of her forehead.

"Why not?"

"How do we explain the fact that I killed Adam?" I whisper.

Montana's eyes widen. "I didn't think about that... So, no police then," she agrees. "I don't think I can see her, Luke."

"You won't have to. I'll go and see her." I leave out the part that when I do see her, I'm going to ensure she can never hurt Montana again. I don't care what I have to do to make certain of that.

"Do you think my dad knew? Where she went?" Montana asks. "I don't understand why someone would leave their family and start a new one somewhere else, obviously a fucked-up one, but still."

"I don't know if your dad knows. I think that your mom is mentally unstable, Tanna. Normal people don't go around agreeing to sacrifice their children." I clear my throat and force a weak smile. "Let's pack a bag. Gray will be here soon."

We're leaving now. I didn't want to sleep on this. As soon as we found out where her mother was, I wanted to leave. I need to put an end to this shit. If

Sean had come to me with all this instead of heading out on his own, I could have stopped it. I could have stopped him from killing himself. Thinking that would save his sister. Unfortunately, time machines don't exist, and I can't go back and change history.

"What do you pack for the *I'm going on a road trip with two mafia families* adventure?" Montana laughs. It sounds off. I can tell she's nervous.

"They're not bad people, Tanna. They're our friends," I remind her. I've had longer to get used to Gray's world, and what that entails. Not that his family ever really bothered me. They seem pretty normal when you get to know them.

"I know. But seriously, Luke, what do I pack?" she asks, staring into the closet that's slowly filling up with her clothes. New clothes.

"Whatever you want to pack," I say. "It doesn't matter what you wear, Tanna."

She huffs. "How long do you think we'll be gone?"

"Plan for two days, max."

"Okay." Montana walks into the closet, coming back out five minutes later with her arms full of hangers.

I raise an eyebrow at her. "That's how you pack for two days?"

"I didn't know what I'd need." She dumps the pile onto the bed.

Without saying anything, I grab an overnight bag that matches the one I've already packed for myself and set it next to her pile. "You won't need this much, Tanna. It's just two days."

"What if it takes longer?"

"Then we'll buy more clothes," I say, lifting a shoulder.

"That's just wasting money. We already have so many clothes."

I watch as she folds her stuff, filling the bag with as much as possible before zipping it shut. She couldn't fit the entire pile inside but, surprisingly, she managed to get a lot of it in that little bag.

"When we get there, I don't want you going anywhere alone. I want you to always have someone with you. If it's not me, then preferably someone from Gray's team or one of Liliana's cousins," I tell her.

"I won't go anywhere alone. I'm not reckless, Luke. I want the dream, remember? Our dream. If my mother wants to drain me of my blood, I'm not going to make it easy for her by handing myself over on a silver platter."

"Thank you." I take both bags and walk downstairs just as Gray pushes through the front door.

"You lovebirds ready to hit the road?" he asks, his voice way too fucking cheery.

"Ready," Montana says.

"Great, let's do this." Gray holds the door open for us, pulling it shut as soon as we're through.

"Uncle Luke, Uncle Luke!" Graycee calls out, running up the footpath and barreling towards me.

I drop the bags on the ground to catch her. "Graycee!" I yell back, matching her excitement.

"You and Daddy are going on a trip," she says. "You're supposed to say goodbye to me first."

"I was just heading over to do that. You beat me to it." I hug her tight. When I set Graycee back on her feet, she gives me that look that tells me she doesn't buy my bullshit.

"Mama says Montana is my auntie now. 'Cause you got married."

"I did," I tell her.

"I like having aunties." Graycee grins. "Auntie Aliyah says that aunties are better than uncles."

I place a hand over my heart. "No way. I don't believe that. I thought I was your favorite, Graycee."

"Mmm, I think Uncle Liam is," she deadpans.

Well, way to bruise my ego, kid.

"Graycee, baby, we have to go." Gray walks in and scoops up his daughter. "And you have homework to do, remember?"

"I remember." Graycee nods.

"I'll see you when I get back, Graycee," I call after them. Then pick up the bags and head towards the car with Montana.

Chapter Thirty-Seven

There are so many people. Personally, I think it's a bit much. I mean, we're talking about an unstable woman who's out to get me here. Not an army. I've been trying to feel something for my mom. I've been replaying memories from a time when she was actually a mother to me.

I loved her. Back then, she did everything that a mother should do. She was loving, caring. And then one day she decided she didn't want that anymore. I don't get it. I'm tempted to ask Luke if I can go with him. To see her. I want to ask her why I wasn't enough. Why Sean wasn't enough... What made her go and find a new family...

I wish I didn't have these questions. And I know the reality of getting the answers is slim. Then again, maybe I'm better off not knowing? I mean, the truth isn't always freeing. Sometimes it hurts more than the unknown.

"I've raided the vending machine." Aliyah drops an armful of snacks onto the bed. We arrived at the hotel an hour ago. Luke and Gray went with some of the guys who work for the Monroes to the farm where my mother is supposed to be.

Somehow, Liliana's cousins managed to close off the rest of our floor at the hotel. They have security posted at all the exits as well as surrounding the outside of the building.

"Thanks," I say, picking up a chocolate bar.

"You know, it took me a really long time to realize that I wasn't the reason my mother insane. You're not the reason yours is either," Aliyah says, then adds, "I feel like we're kindred spirits, sisters in another life or something."

"Kindred spirits?"

"We both have fucked-up mothers who wanted us dead." She smiles, but there's a sadness in her eyes.

"I just couldn't imagine ever wanting to hurt someone in my family. When I have a child, I'm certain I'll want to protect them. Keep them away from anything that could harm them. How could a mother do this to her own child?" I ask her.

"I don't know. Maybe it's not them. Maybe they're possessed by some evil demon or something? No one knows why some people are totally zen and others are unstable. It's just life. And as shitty as the cards that you've been dealt are, you are stronger for it. You've survived a lot, Montana. And this? It's going to make you question a lot, but don't let it derail what you've already achieved."

"I don't know what I'd do without you. You really have been so kind and just... accepting of me."

"Because I'm amazing, obviously. But amazing can recognize amazing. The moment I saw you, I knew you were an awesome person."

"You *are* amazing." I bite into the candy bar.

"And you bring chocolate. Which makes you even more amazing."

The door opens and Liliana, Travis, and Liam walk into my room. "You started a party without me? Rude," Liliana says with a fake scowl on her face.

"You're late. So who's the rude one?" Aliyah counters. "And these are not for you." She points an accusatory finger at her husband.

"What did I ever do to you to deserve this torture, Mrs. King? I can't go the next sixty years without snacks, babe." Liam sits on the bed, his arms crossed and an exaggerated pout on his face.

"Only sixty years?" Aliyah laughs. "Liam, I'm going to find you in heaven, and even then, I'll monitor your sugar intake."

"You should let him have a snack, Lia. He gets grumpy if he goes too long without a sugar burst," Travis says.

"Okay, fine. Liam King, you can eat whatever snacks you want. But you're bunking with O'Neil. I'm not staying awake all night dealing with your hyperactive brain when you're trying to burn off that sugar high."

"That's not happening," Travis growls, snatching a packet of cookies out of Liam's hands.

"You really get hyperactive?" I ask Liam. I mean, can the guy get any more extra than he already is?

"No," Liam says, at the same time everyone else responds with a solid, "Yes."

"Well, okay then. I'd totally give you snacks, but Aliyah's the boss," I tell Liam.

"A hot boss." He grins before snatching her up. "We'll be right back. My wife and I need to have words," Liam says before walking out the door with a disgruntled Aliyah in his arms.

"They won't be back anytime soon." Liliana laughs.

"It's okay. More snacks for us." I hold up another chocolate bar, offering it to her.

"Thanks. I like your thinking," she says.

"I'm gonna head back to our room, babe. Call me if you need anything." Travis kisses Liliana before walking out.

"And then there were two." Liliana taps her chocolate bar against mine as if we were holding champagne glasses instead of sweets.

I reach for the remote, flick on the television, and scroll until I find a sappy Hallmark movie. I don't know how long Luke is going to be, but I want to try to be awake when he gets back.

I wake up to whispered voices. Opening my eyes, I see two males talking to each other at the door. Luke and Gray. I look to my left, where Liliana was sitting, but the bed is empty, bar all the snack wrappers we left scattered around.

Shit. I need to clean the mess. Luke shouldn't have to come back to this giant mess. I push up and start collecting the trash, my hands a frenzied rush to make sure I get them all.

I look up when I hear the door close, and Luke walks towards me. "I'm sorry. I'm sorry. I fell asleep. I didn't mean to. I'm cleaning it up," I rush out. I can feel the panic rising within me.

"It's okay. I've got it, Tanna." Luke collects whatever I didn't grab and then reaches out and takes the bits I'm holding in my hands. He dumps everything into the trash can before yanking his shirt over his head.

My gaze catches on my name scripted across his ribs. I've seen it a million times now, but that doesn't change how amazed I am that he actually did that for me. A little bit of the panic settles in my chest. "I really am sorry," I tell him.

Luke gets into bed. He pulls the covers back and shifts until he's right next to me. "Come on, lie down. It's late, Tanna," he says. I climb in next to him and scoot my body against his. "I love you." He kisses me briefly. "Always."

"I love you," I tell him. "What happened? At the farm? Did you see her?"

"I did. But we didn't go in. I watched from outside for a bit. We decided to go back tomorrow. There were a lot of people there. Gray's called his father and he's sending a few more guys up here."

"Is it dangerous, Luke? I don't want you to put yourself in harm's way for me."

"It's not dangerous. I'll be fine. I'm going to talk to your mom. Get her to stop all this ritual bullshit and let her know that she's not ever going to get to you," he says.

I'm not stupid. I know he's going to kill her or *someone* is going to kill her. Luke won't just let her keep plotting and planning. I'm not a hundred percent sure how I feel about knowing that my mother is going to die.

If I'm being honest with myself, she died a long time ago to me. I don't have a relationship with her, and I don't want one anymore. That doesn't mean I'm not saddened by it though. I want that life I dreamed of having, and I'm not going to let anything or anybody stop me from having it.

I've been weak long enough. It's time for me to be stronger. To fight for the life I want to have. Not just accept the shitty hand I was dealt. If Luke is prepared to fight this much for me, then I'll do the same. Because he's worth it. *We're* worth it.

Chapter Thirty-Eight

I'm keen to get this over with. I want to go back to Vancouver and start my fucking life with Montana. These past couple of weeks have been a nightmare. I'm still having flashbacks of seeing my wife's lifeless body in my arms. That's not something I ever want to experience again.

There are five SUVs. I'm in one with Gray and his brother, Vinny. My knee bounces. I want to get this done. I wouldn't say I enjoy taking a life, considering I've only ever done it once before, and it's not something I plan on continuing.

But it's a necessity. My need to keep Montana safe makes it worth the risk of whatever could happen to me. Her life is more important to me than anything else. If I have to spend the rest of my years behind bars, knowing that the assholes determined to hurt her are no longer breathing, then I'm okay with that.

We pull up the long winding road on the farmland the cult uses as their base of operation.

"Let me get out first. Let me talk to her first," Vinny says.

"Why?" I ask him.

"Because she knows you, and we don't want to spook her," he explains. "Let me get her restrained so she can't run off, and then I'll signal for you to come out."

I nod my head in agreement, when really it's the last thing I want to do. If she runs, I can fucking chase her ass. I don't care about the extra effort. That said, I will do this his way. I'm not exactly the expert on turning up at someone's residence with a plan to kill them.

"It's going to work out," Gray tells me.

"I know." I'm not leaving here without knowing that woman's heart no longer beats within her chest.

Vinny gets out of the car, followed by a bunch of his guys, and together they all approach the perimeter. Gray waits in the back of the SUV with me. I don't know if it's for moral support or if it's more to make sure I don't jump out.

It doesn't take long before Vinny and his guys are surrounded by a crowd of people. Other cult members, I'm guessing. "Fucking morons," Gray mumbles under his breath while staring through the windshield.

Everyone is wearing some shade of white or cream. It's the very picture of one of those weird communes you see on documentaries, right before everyone drinks the Kool-Aid. I look through the many faces. But I don't see hers. I don't see the man she's supposed to be married to either.

I studied the photos of the pair of them for hours. Then again after we surveilled the farm yesterday. I wanted to know them the moment I saw them. But they're not here, among the group of people surrounding Vinny and his guys, who are all pointing guns at them. Not that the cult members seem at all fazed by the weapons aimed their way.

None of them are saying anything. They're just looking. Staring. Almost as if they're seeing aliens or some shit. It's weird, and a little freaky. "What the fuck is going on?" I ask Gray.

"No idea." He shrugs.

"They're not here," I tell him while gesturing out the window. That's when I see it. A blur, someone shuffling through the tents. "There!" I point, not waiting for Gray to acknowledge me before I open the door and run in that direction.

I weave around the tents. I can see two figures ahead of me. I can't tell if it's them, but my gut is telling me I'm right. Spineless fuckers. Some leaders they are. Running at the sign of trouble and leaving their unsuspecting minions to face the firing squad. Quite literally.

I catch up to the pair, tackling the first one I can to the ground. A grunt is followed by a string of curse words as I land on top of him. Then someone is pounding on my back repeatedly. "Get off him. What the hell do you think you're doing?" a female voice hisses at me.

I look over my shoulder and recognition hits both of us. I jump off the figure on the ground, just as Gray stops short, pulls the guy to his feet, and holds him in place. I take two steps towards Kristy Baker. My mother-in-law. The bitch who wants to kill my wife.

"Luke? What are you doing here?" she asks. "How's your mother?"

"You know exactly why I'm here, Kristy." I don't owe her the same respect I did as a child. I won't call her ma'am or Mrs. Baker. She's just Kristy now. And she doesn't even deserve that.

"No, I don't." She shakes her head while taking a step backwards.

"You see, I heard you've been after my wife. You want to sacrifice Montana for your own selfish agenda," I tell her what she already knows.

"Your wife? You and Montana got married? When?" Kristy folds her arms over her chest, not doing a single thing to refute the claims I just made.

"That would be something I'd share with her mother. But you? You're not her mother. You're nothing but a pathetic excuse for a human being. Do you have any idea how much your leaving fucked them up?" I'm angry. I don't know if I've ever hated a person as much as I hate her right now. Except maybe Andrew. They can share the privilege.

"I'm her mother, and this is her birthright. It's an honor to be the sacrifice. She'll see that," Kristy says.

"You don't get it. I'm not here to have a friendly little chat. I'm here to make sure you can never hurt my wife again," I tell her.

I pull the pistol out from where it was tucked into the waistband of my pants. It seems I still have some morals when it comes to this woman, because I can't bring myself to fucking hit her. Instead, I aim the barrel right between her eyes.

"Any other mother would be fucking proud of her. She's an amazing person, despite what you've done to her. But you'll never know that." I click the safety off and press down on the trigger. My arm jerks back slightly. "I'll see you in hell," I grunt as Kristy's body hits the ground.

"No! You can't. What did you do?" This comes from her husband.

Vinny steps forward and takes the gun out of my hands. "Go get in the car," he says before turning to his brother. "Gray, take him home. I'm going to finish up here."

"Come on. Let's get out of here." Gray lands a

palm on my shoulder, and I follow him to the car before jumping into the passenger seat.

Throughout the drive, Gray keeps glancing in my direction. I have no idea what he's looking for, but I don't say a single thing. When we're thirty minutes away from the hotel, he stops the car on the side of the road and pivots to face me. "You okay?"

"Fine," I tell him. "Why wouldn't I be?"

"Because you just shot your mother-in-law?"

"That was not Montana's mother. That woman hasn't deserved that title in a really long time," I say. "I'm not going to let anyone who's a threat to my wife continue to breathe the same air as her."

"Okay. Well, if you ever need to talk or anything, you know I'm here." He pulls back into traffic.

"I appreciate that."

When we park at the hotel, Gray heads to his room and I go straight for mine. Montana is sitting cross-legged on the bed watching a movie. She looks at me and then jumps up.

Without a word, she walks over and throws her arms around my waist. "Thank you," she whispers.

"You don't have to thank me, Tanna." I kiss the top of her head.

"Are you okay?" She peers up at me.

"I am now that you're in my arms. Are you ready to go home? We have a dream to start living."

"More than ready," Montana says. "I love you, Luke, so much."

"I love you." I lean in and press my lips to hers. This woman is my whole fucking world. I was an idiot for wasting so many years without her. I will never spend another day away from her.

Epilogue

A Year and Some Months Later

I pick up my daughter and place her in the baby carrier that's strapped to my chest. I can tell Montana doesn't really want to leave Aubrey with Aliyah and King, and I'm not going to force her to take that step. I'm also not opposed to having my daughter attached to me. I planned this dinner for Montana. I wanted to spend some time with her. Away from everyone else. Just the two of us. Or the *three* of us.

Aubrey is perfect, though. She doesn't even stir as I tighten the straps. She snuggles against me and falls right back to sleep. I remember the day Montana told me she was pregnant. We'd been trying for a few months. *Actively trying*. Something I was more than willing to participate in.

I loved a pregnant Montana, and I can't wait to get her knocked up again. In exactly two years.

"Hey, I thought we were leaving her?" Montana says, walking out of the bathroom and taking my fucking breath away. She's wearing a white sundress that reaches her ankles and hangs low across her chest.

I inhale as my eyes rake up and down her body. My wife is a goddamn siren. "I changed my mind." I note her instant relief. Her whole body relaxes, which tells me I made the right call. "You ready?" I ask while holding out a hand.

"Always." Montana places her palm in mine and we walk out of the bedroom together.

"Hey, guys. I've had a change of heart. I'm

keeping my daughter, and you two are going to have to work on getting your own kid," I tell Aliyah and King.

"No fucking way!" Gray grunts from the kitchen. Everyone shares a laugh, except my best friend, who's staring daggers at the back of his brother-in-law's head.

I turn to Montana. "Let's get out of here before World War III breaks out when Monroe notices his little sister is actually a married woman," I whisper.

"Sounds like a good idea," she says.

I guide Montana out through the back door, where I had the garden set up with an intimate dinner. There are lights and flowers everywhere. Okay, I might not have done it all myself. Aliyah and Liliana helped out a lot. I'm still taking the credit, though.

"This is so beautiful, Luke," Montana says, her wide eyes trying to take it all in.

"Not nearly half as beautiful as my two girls," I reply before pulling out her chair. "Come on, sit down."

"I love you," Montana tells me over the table as I take the seat opposite her.

"I love you."

"Thank you for doing this."

"I know we haven't really had a lot of date nights lately and I'm sorry for that, babe."

"It's not your fault, Luke. We're just busy. We have a baby and you had the playoffs."

"It's not okay. I love our date nights, Tanna. I'm not giving them up. We're just going to have to be more creative when it comes to scheduling time for us. Because nothing is more important than us. You, Aubrey, and me. This life and the next, right?"

"This life and the next," Montana repeats.

Have you joined my Reader's group? Come and hang out with other KK readers in Club Merge!!!

Also by Kylie Kent

The Merge Series

Merged With Him (Zac and Alyssa's Story)

Fused With Him (Bray and Reilly's Story)

Entwined With Him (Dean and Ella's Story)

2nd Generation Merge Series

Ignited by Him (Ash and Breanna's Story)

An Entangled Christmas: A Merge Series Christmas
Novel (Alex and Lily's Story)

Chased By him (Chase and Hope's Story)

Tethered To Him (Noah and Ava's Story)

Seattle Soulmates

Her List (Axel and Amalia's Story)

McKinley's Obsession Duet

Josh and Emily's Story

Ruining Her

Ruining Him

Sick Love Duet

Dom and Lucy's Story

Unhinged Desires

Certifiable Attraction

The Valentino Empire

Devilish King (Holly and Theo's Story)

Unassuming Queen (Holly and Theo's Story)

United Reign (Holly and Theo's Story)

Brutal Princess (Neo and Angelica's Story)

Reclaiming Lola (Lola and Dr James's Story)

Sons of Valentino Series

Relentless Devil (Theo and Maddie's Story)

Merciless Devil (Matteo and Savannah's Story)

Soulless Devil (Romeo and Livvy's Story)

Reckless Devil (Luca and Katarina's Story)

A Valentino Reunion (The Entire Valentino Crime Family)

The Tempter Series

Following His Rules (Xavier and Shardonnay's Story)

Following His Orders (Nathan and Bentley's Story)

Following His Commands (Alistair and Dani's Story)

Legacy of Valentino

Izzy and Mikhail's Story

Remorseless Devilette

Vengeful Devilette

Vancouver Knights Series

Break Out (Liam and Aliyah's Story)

Know The Score (Grayson and Kathryn's Story)

Light It Up Red (Travis and Liliana's Story)

Puck Blocked (Luke and Montana's Story)

De Bellis Crime Family

A Sinner's Promise (Gio and Eloise's Story)

A Sinner's Lies (Gabe and Daisy's Story)

A Sinner's Virtue (Marcel and Zoe's Story)

A Sinner's Saint (Vin and Cammi's Story)

A Sinner's Truth (Santo and Aria's Story)

About the Author

Kylie made the leap from kindergarten teacher to romance author, living out her dream to deliver sexy, always and forever romances. She loves a happily ever after story with tons of built-in steam.

She currently resides in Perth, Australia and when she is not dreaming up the latest romance, she can be found spending time with her three children and her husband of twenty years, her very own real-life, instant love.

Kylie loves to hear from her readers. You can reach her at: author.kylie.kent@gmail.com

Let's stay in touch. Come and hang out in my readers group on Facebook, and follow me on instagram.